"Why are you helping me?" she asked with a lost quality to her voice. The sound was the equivalent to a knife stab to the chest.

"Because I can and it's the right thing to do," he admitted. It was the truth. No one would accuse him of being perfect but he would never turn his back on someone who needed help.

"You seem to have caught on to something law enforcement hasn't put together yet. What is it?" she continued after a quick nod.

"I just don't see you dragging a body from the trunk of your car to the spot where it was buried. The victim would have had to walk there himself and then climb in the grave," he stated as honestly as he could. Plus, her vulnerability tugged at his heart.

"Do you recognize my last name?" she asked with a raised eyebrow.

He had to think about that one. *Cantor.*

Realization dawned.

TEXAS SCANDAL

USA TODAY Bestselling Author

BARB HAN

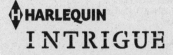

All my love to Brandon, Jacob and Tori, who are the great loves of my life. To Samantha for the bright shining light that you are.

To Babe, my hero, for being my best friend, greatest love and my place to call home. I love you with everything that I am. Always and forever.

Recycling programs for this product may not exist in your area.

ISBN-13: 978-1-335-59043-5

Texas Scandal

Harlequin Enterprises ULC
22 Adelaide St. West, 41st Floor
Toronto, Ontario M5H 4E3, Canada
www.Harlequin.com

Printed in U.S.A.

USA TODAY bestselling author **Barb Han** lives
in north Texas with her very own hero-worthy
husband, three beautiful children, a spunky golden
retriever/standard poodle mix and too many books
in her to-read pile. In her downtime, she plays video
games and spends much of her time on or around a
basketball court. She loves interacting with readers
and is grateful for their support. You can reach her
at barbhan.com.

Books by Barb Han

Harlequin Intrigue

The Cowboys of Cider Creek

Rescued by the Rancher
Riding Shotgun
Trapped in Texas
Texas Scandal

A Ree and Quint Novel

Undercover Couple
Newlywed Assignment
Eyewitness Man and Wife
Mission Honeymoon

An O'Connor Family Mystery

Texas Kidnapping
Texas Target
Texas Law
Texas Baby Conspiracy
Texas Stalker
Texas Abduction

Visit the Author Profile page at Harlequin.com.

CAST OF CHARACTERS

Melody Cantor—Tagged as a murderer, but will she end up the next victim?

Tiernan Hayes—When a dead body shows up on his property, how far will he go to find the real killer?

Henry Cooper Cantor III, aka Coop—Melody's brother is determined to protect family secrets.

Jason Riker—Why was this eighteen-year-old holding Melody's address in his hand at the time of his murder?

Bebe Riker—What will she do to avenge her son's murder?

Sheriff Cleve Tanner—Is he inept at his job or downright dirty?

Chapter One

Tiernan Hayes stood on the steps of his back porch and whistled. Loki, his black Lab mix who was all heart and every kind of trouble, had chased after a squirrel and disappeared into the scrub brush. Since the one-year-old rescue had given chase to a rabbit yesterday and come home reeking of skunk spray, Tiernan didn't have time for a repeat performance. *Not two days in a row.*

"Loki," he shouted as he jogged across the small yard toward the wooded area on his property. He owned as far as the eye could see and then some. His decade on the rodeo circuit might've given his body every crick and groan, but it had also made him enough money to start a custom saddle business and buy his own four-acre piece of the Lone Star State. Not too bad if anyone asked him.

He listened for Loki's heavy breathing or the sound of twigs breaking as he bolted across the scrub. Something moved deeper into the trees and to the clearing. The back of his property backed up to a farm road. Even though there was little traffic, he still worried Loki would run in front of a truck. The animal was bright. That wasn't the problem. He was curious and had way too much puppy inside him to make good decisions. Any Lab owner would agree that it took about five years for them to settle down enough to become the best dog anyone could hope to own.

One down. Four to go. But who was counting?

Tiernan had a busy day ahead. Orders were stacking up. His brothers had reached out to tell him to come home to the family cattle ranch his grandfather had built from scratch. Duncan Hayes was the reason Tiernan had left Cider Creek after high school graduation. The man had been a bear. His grandfather's recent death from heat exhaustion had weighed heavy on Tiernan's heart, since his mother was left to work the multimillion-dollar operation on her own. She had requested everyone come home for an announcement. A couple of Tiernan's brothers made the trip and deemed it necessary for everyone to follow suit. If Tiernan could get ahead of his orders, he would make the trip. At this rate, he was looking at the New Year before he could wrap up all the Christmas presents on order. He didn't have it in his heart for a young rider to be disappointed at the holidays.

In fact, he'd taken on too much after a few parents begged. The money would come in handy, too. He never took for granted the fact he was building his business—a business based on his success on the circuit. He was developing a reputation by delivering high-quality custom saddles on time.

Since there was still no sign of Loki, Tiernan headed deeper into the thicket. He whistled again without any luck. This dog was determined to make Tiernan work for it today. Hells bells. The clock was ticking, and he was already pulling eighteen-hour days in the small shop he'd built behind his log-cabin-style home. Everyone had told him that he could set his own hours as an entrepreneur, and yet he worked all of them anyway.

Growing up working a cattle ranch had given him the right skills to survive. Calving season, which ran from January to March at Hayes Cattle, had taught him how to go days without sleep.

His boot caught on a vine. He narrowly escaped a face-plant by grabbing hold of the closest tree trunk, a mesquite. Pain shot through his right shoulder with contact. When he brought his gaze up, he saw movement ahead in a small clearing. Wind gusted, sending a stench that hit

Tiernan so hard it nearly doubled him over. Bile burned the back of his throat at the smell of rotting meat with a tinge of sweetness to it. He was familiar with the scent.

Loki was digging where Tiernan guessed was the source of the smell. A dead animal shouldn't be buried.

"Loki," he said in more of a commanding than casual tone. "Come."

Loki's ears perked up. He craned his neck around, locked on to Tiernan and then bolted toward him. The dog had two speeds—full-on assault as he gunned toward Tiernan and passed-out-on-the-floor mode, usually belly up.

Tiernan fished his cell phone out of his back pocket. He checked the bars to make sure he had service before calling 911.

"Fire, sheriff or ambulance?" the female voice asked on the other end of the line.

"Sheriff," he confirmed.

"What's the nature of this call?" the dispatcher asked after introducing herself as Helen.

"Based on the smell and the fact there's a fresh grave, I suspect there's a dead body buried on my property," Tiernan said. He knew better than to tamper with a site that might be considered a crime scene. He'd tracked enough dangerous poachers in his younger years and worked with enough law enforcement to know how important preserving a crime scene could be to an investigation.

Of course, he hoped like hell he was wrong about the dead body. Years of experience said he wasn't.

"What's your location, sir?" Helen asked.

A twig snapped to the left. Loki caught sight of something moving, so naturally he took off toward it.

"Loki," Tiernan scolded. It was too late. The dog had selective hearing when he locked on to a target, and he'd already disappeared into the thicket. Tiernan bit back a curse.

"Sir?" Helen said.

"Sorry." Tiernan turned to follow Loki as it occurred to him a murderer might still be on his land. Since he hadn't been expecting anything in the neighborhood of chasing down a cold-blooded killer, his Colt 45 was inside his workshop. It came in handy when there were coyotes around.

He gave his location and told Helen where a deputy could find him. Then, he stayed on the line with her until Deputy Calhoun arrived on the scene.

"I'm Tiernan Hayes," he said to the deputy before extending a hand. Calhoun gave a firm shake. "My dog caught a scent and ended up here." He motioned toward the site, wondering if he'd ever get the putrid smell out of his nose.

Calhoun walked over to the fresh grave after tying a bandana around his face to cover his nose. A small shovel extended from his left hand. Digging lasted less than two minutes before he glanced over and then nodded, confirming there was a dead body inside.

As FAR AS thick gray clouds went, the ones slowly rolling across the Austin sky hinted at a gloom and doom kind of day. Melody Cantor walked to her sedan, light in her step despite Mother Nature's somber mood. The job interview had gone well, and an offer was promised, meaning she would be able to put in her notice at the soul-sucking job where she presently worked for one of the wealthiest men in Texas. At thirty-three, she was starting to realize how fast time flew. Wasting another day as the right hand of real estate tycoon Byron Hunter, with his endless demands and sparse compensation by comparison, wasn't worth it. Melody had drawn the line when he'd looked the other way while his firstborn son made an inappropriate pass at a Give Thanks–themed open house two weeks ago. There was nothing to be grateful for while she was trying to fight off Spence Hunter, who'd seemed determined to keep her from climbing down from the ladder she'd been on.

If luck was on her side, the offer from Community Planners would be waiting in her email inbox by the time she arrived home. The company was much larger than the family-owned operation where she currently worked.

A white slip of paper fluttered like a bird trapped in a cage on the windshield of her Camry. A parking ticket? Melody bit back a curse and denied this could be an omen.

As she neared her vehicle, which she'd wedged into what she believed was a legal spot, she realized the paper was too wide to be a ticket. A note? Was someone cursing her out for taking a spot that belonged to them?

Great. Just great.

Melody snatched the paper from her windshield and flattened the note onto the hood of her car.

Drive fifty miles west.

Right now? Was this a prank? She glanced up and down the street, unsure of exactly who or what she was looking for. Someone laughing? Someone staring? Someone paying special attention to her now that she'd read the message? No one seemed to notice her or care, but it was impossible to see everything. Someone could be hiding.

A cold shiver raced up her spine as she reread the chicken scratch handwriting. What was fifty miles from her current location? This had to be a misunderstanding or some kind of practical joke.

Melody reached inside her handbag and located the key fob. She palmed it and then clicked the unlock button. Camrys weren't exactly rare. This note being placed on hers was probably a mistake.

She took the driver's seat and then closed the door behind her.

What if it wasn't, though? She locked the door before grabbing her cell phone to check Google Maps. From her location, fifty miles west of Austin would put her in Blanco, Johnson City or Meadowlakes. Just shy of those would put her in Marble Falls or possibly Shovel Mountain. Since she didn't know anyone who lived in any of those cities, she crumpled up the note and tossed it onto the passenger seat, determined not to let the cryptic message ruin her post-interview high.

Besides, it wasn't a ticket, which was no small miracle considering parking in Austin was almost as confusing as sitting in on her employer's meetings with his accountant at tax time.

A thought struck as Melody navigated out of the parking spot where she was sandwiched between a red Tesla and a Ducati motorcycle.

Could this somehow be related to her father? After all, he was in prison awaiting trial for mail fraud. He'd convinced a whole lot of folks they'd be better off handing over their money to "get in on the ground floor" of his new business opportunity. An investigation into his business operations turned up even more charges.

The scheme he'd initially been busted for turned out to be the tip of the iceberg on his illegal dealings. But walking in on her father while he was cheating on her mother with Melody's favorite high school English teacher in her office had shattered all her beliefs about growing up in what she'd once believed was the perfect family.

When it came to Henry Cooper Cantor II, her attitude was more like, *What has he done now?* Her brother, Henry Cooper Cantor III, who went by Coop, worked for their father and claimed the man was innocent. Evidence didn't seem to agree. Melody had walked away from the family drama after catching her dad with his pants down years ago. She'd donated her trust fund to feed the hungry and never looked back. Now, she wished she had kept some so she could repay at least a portion of the money her father had taken from others. The thought of all those lavish birthday parties during her childhood that must have been funded by her father swindling other people out of their cash almost made her sick. Did it make her a target?

Fifty miles west? Was someone waiting out there for her to show up? A murderer? A rapist? Since her current line of thought had taken her to a dark place, she took in a slow, deep breath to hit the mental reset button.

The note creeped her out more than she wanted to admit.

"Call Coop's cell," she said to her phone after speaking the magic words to get its attention. Through some magic of Bluetooth technology, the call started ringing through her stereo speakers. She wondered if anyone even called them stereo speakers anymore. If not, what would the new name be? Car speakers made it simple enough.

"You okay?" Coop asked, sounding more than a little caught off guard by the random call. Granted, she could be better about keeping in touch. Since her parents' divorce, the four of them no longer spent holidays together, let alone have regular conversations. There were no more birthday parties or Sunday brunch tables for four. Her mother, Tilly, had drawn a line in the sand that said she wanted out of all activities that involved her ex. The term *coparenting* was a joke when it came to her mother's perspective on their former family. Thankfully,

Melody and Coop had been old enough to take care of themselves.

"Fine," she said, realizing she sounded the opposite.

"Is it Dad?" he asked.

"No," she countered, feeling a little defensive at the abrasiveness in his tone.

"Then what?" he asked.

"Am I not allowed to call and check on my brother?" she asked, feeling every bit the hypocrite. He wasn't too far off base. Lately, neither one called the other unless there was something to do with their father's case. Usually, it was more bad news.

He didn't respond.

"Okay, you got me," she said. "I don't call just to check on you but that doesn't mean I don't care or think about you."

The truth was that she'd basically cut herself off from the family when she dumped her trust fund into Austin-area food banks. Her father had flipped out and her brother had called her delusional for thinking money grew on trees. He couldn't begin to fathom why she might not want Cantor money or wasn't bursting with pride to have the Cantor name.

Melody never once looked back after getting rid of the trust. Her brother had lost most of his betting on the stock market, thinking he could double it. So, he'd gone to work for their father to rebuild his personal wealth and she'd worked at ordinary jobs they all thumbed their noses at.

The reason for the tension in her brother's voice dawned on her. If her father was involved in illegal activity, wouldn't it stand to reason Coop had been, as well? At the very least, he had to have known about the criminal activity. The question was whether or not he was an accomplice or simply looked the other way.

"Are you doing okay, Coop?" she asked. "I mean, about everything?"

"There's no reason not to be," he countered a little too quickly. "Dad will beat this because he didn't do anything wrong. This is a witch hunt, nothing more."

"You said the exact same words the last time we spoke several weeks ago ever since Dad has been in jail," she said. As much as she wanted to believe those words, there was far too much evidence to the contrary to be that naive or blindly loyal.

"Because they're true," Coop shot back. His defensiveness was on full display, coming through loud and clear on the line.

"And you?" she asked. "You didn't answer my question about how you're doing."

"Dad is in jail," he said with an accusatory tone. "How am I supposed to feel?"

"I guess that's a fair point," she reasoned, figuring this call was a mistake. Her brother would go to his grave defending their father. He'd treated her like the enemy after she freaked out over the man cheating years ago. Coop had made it seem like she was the reason the family had broken apart and their mother resented everything about her relationship with their father. As though witnessing her father's infidelity hadn't been soul crushing enough for Melody, the backlash was somehow her fault.

"I took a few days off and headed out of town to get my head straight," he said. Coop had always lived in a fantasy world of his own making. Reality didn't seem to have a place once he'd made up his mind on a subject. Words like *facts* and *evidence* had no bearing after Coop decided on their father's innocence.

"Sounds like a good idea," she said. A piece of Melody wished she had the ability to turn a blind eye to reality. Maybe then she would be a lot happier. Knowing the truth was awful on a lot of levels when it came to realizing her father wasn't the person she'd believed he was for all those early years.

Hoping to make a quick pit stop at home to change out of her interview clothes, she saw a law enforcement vehicle on her street. What was going on?

There was a man sitting in the passenger seat of the SUV. He was better looking than anyone had a right to be. She didn't recognize him. When he made eye contact, a trill of awareness shot through her despite the ominous scene unfolding.

For a split second, she thought about ditching the clothing change idea to avoid the hassle of going inside the apartment while something was going down. Work wasn't far from here. Although, the thought of going into the office right now held no appeal. Besides, it might be better to find out what was up.

As she pulled into the spot where she usually parked at her above the garage apartment, the SUV pulled in right behind her, blocking her exit. Awareness was quickly replaced with fear as one of Austin PD's finest came walking up to the driver's side, right hand resting on the butt of the gun strapped to his hip.

"Coop, I have to go," she said before ending the call and steeling herself for whatever was about to happen.

Chapter Two

"Ma'am, is your name Melody Cantor?" Deputy Calhoun asked as Tiernan watched and listened from the front seat of the deputy's SUV. He'd been warned the stop would be recorded before the deputy turned the camera on. It was routine, he'd said. From the moment the body had been found to now, Tiernan wasn't certain if Melody Cantor was a witness or a suspect. Based on the camera being turned on to record what was happening, his mind snapped to the latter.

Tiernan couldn't get a good look at the driver from this vantage point. The glimpse he'd gotten of her as she drove past had stirred up a foreign feeling in his chest along with a jolt of attraction. She shifted and a pair of worried eyes glanced into the rearview. Hers were a deep shade of brown. Long, russet hair fell down her back in waves as she stepped out of her vehicle.

A thorough investigation would fill in the fine print of the report. But looking at her right off the bat he wondered how someone of her size and stature could have bludgeoned a young man, lifted his dead weight, and then managed to bury him. Very little blood was found on his clothing according to the deputy, and the victim been covered with a blanket.

Since part of Tiernan's property backed up to a farm road and all indications pointed toward the body entering his property from there, he acknowledged the perp wouldn't have had far to go to get to the burial site. The loss of life hit Tiernan as a gut punch.

Still, this woman didn't fit any of his preconceived notions of a murderer. Plus, hadn't he been told or read somewhere along the way women normally used poison and not brute strength to commit murder?

Deputy Calhoun didn't slap cuffs on her, so that was another good sign she was being treated as a witness for now. The lawman had balked at first when Tiernan had asked to ride along. Dropping the last name Hayes to the sheriff had given Tiernan an advantage. Under normal circumstances, he wouldn't think of using his family's stature for special treatment. As a citizen, he had a right to know what was going on. As a former rancher, he was protective of his land. As a human being, he wouldn't rest until he had answers.

There wasn't a whole lot of crime in the small town northeast of Austin where Tiernan lived. He'd chosen Mesquite Spring for its small-town feel and close proximity to the city where he had access to supplies for his business. It didn't hurt matters this location was far away from Fort Worth where his heart had been broken. He had no plans for a repeat performance anytime soon.

"A man has been murdered, ma'am," the deputy said.

"This has to be some kind of misunderstanding," the brunette said with a tinge of worry in her voice. The deputy had left the SUV windows open and it was otherwise quiet outside, so Tiernan could hear the exchange if he strained. "You're welcome to check my trunk right now." She popped the hatch open with the squeeze of her thumb. He'd heard the deputy's first question, whether or not her name was Melody. She must be the person in question because there they were talking and walking toward the back of her vehicle.

"Again, I apologize for the inconvenience and appreciate your cooperation, Ms. Cantor," Deputy Calhoun said before shining a light inside the back of her vehicle. He looked unimpressed and he cut the beam off in less than twenty seconds.

"Go ahead and look again. Search my whole car if you need to," she said on a sharp sigh, her tone a dare. She planted balled fists on her hips. "I can promise you won't find anything no matter how hard you search."

"Has anything unusual occurred recently?" he asked as he moved toward the back seat and repeated the quick look.

"Yes, as a matter of fact it has," she said. Tiernan tried not to notice the way her body curved in a lazy S pattern. Standing next to the deputy, Tiernan would guess her to be five feet seven inches, above the average height and most of it coming from long legs. "I found a note on my windshield after an interview I just had that instructed me to drive fifty miles west."

Even from this distance, Tiernan saw Calhoun's forehead wrinkle in concern with the revelation. Was she being set up or lured somewhere so she could be next?

The victim was male, so Tiernan wasn't making any easy connections. Serial killers were known to target a certain type of person. This didn't add up.

"Can I see the paper?" Calhoun asked.

"I wadded it up and tossed it onto the passenger seat, figuring someone had made a mistake," she stated. "Can I ask a question before I go get it?"

Calhoun nodded.

"What's actually going on?" The trepidation

in her voice made him think she was preparing for the worst, but what did that mean? "Am I under arrest or some kind of suspect? Because I'm confused right now as to what's going on and am starting to believe that I might need to request a lawyer."

"Like I mentioned, there's been a murder, so I'm not at liberty to discuss the details of the case with you," he stated. "All I can say is that your name came up during the investigation."

Melody took a step back as though she'd experienced a physical blow. She dropped her gaze to the concrete like she might find answers there. A few seconds later, she glanced into the SUV's passenger seat and searched his face. Normally, he would smile but this wasn't the time for pleasantries. Plus, the panicked look on her face made it clear she wasn't in the mood.

"How?" she asked, folding her arms across her chest as if creating a barricade between her and the shocking news. She glanced around before quickly continuing, "Why? I mean, this doesn't make any sense. Murder? Who is dead? And where did this happen? How on earth would that be connected to me? I just got out of an interview. You can verify where I've been this morning. Unless..." Her gaze shot up and to the left, like the answers she couldn't find on the concrete might be up there somewhere. Confusion wrinkled her forehead, and his heart went out to her. He was no investigator but she looked like she'd been bowled over by a truck.

"Those are all good questions, ma'am. That's why I'm here, trying to piece together what happened and why," Deputy Calhoun said. "There are a lot of open-ended issues in this case. We're hoping you can provide some information that can close some loops."

"I'm not sure how I'm supposed to do that if you don't tell me who was…" She clamped her mouth shut and closed her eyes.

There was a single slip of paper in the deceased person's pocket. No ID. No wallet. No money. Just a slip of paper with a name and address. Tiernan hadn't gotten a glimpse of the paper and had had to deduce this was the person they were picking up after asking if the deputy could wait while he changed out of the clothes he'd been wearing. Clothes that smelled like death. He never wanted to see those items again, so he'd tossed them in the trash can outside. The deputy had also given a helpful tip to rub a little vapor rub underneath his nose to help overpower the stench. Otherwise, he'd be smelling dead body for several hours, possibly even days. He'd come upon deceased animals before, but they'd never had the kind of impact finding a human being did.

"I'm not sure how I can be of help, but I'll do whatever you need," she finally said.

"Do you mind riding to the sheriff's office with me? We have a few more questions and you might be more comfortable answering them there," Calhoun said as Melody tensed up.

"I'll get the note first," she said before walking around to the passenger side of her vehicle. She retrieved a small piece of paper a little wider than a parking ticket. The city of Austin made their fair share of revenue from the fact parking was a joke downtown. She held the slip out to Calhoun, who asked her to wait a second. He came back to the SUV long enough to retrieve an evidence bag.

Melody dropped it inside with a shocked look on her face. There was no way she was processing everything that was going on. It was evident on her face and the way she stood there, looking lost. A primal protective instinct surged in him at the sight. One that had no business in the middle of a murder investigation. She was innocent. He didn't doubt that one bit. She would have to be one hell of an actress to pull off looking this lost and in shock.

"I have a ride-along passenger today," Calhoun said. "That puts you in back."

"I guess it's settled then," she said, but her tone told him that she wasn't thrilled with the idea.

Tiernan exited the vehicle and held the door open. "Why don't you take my seat? I don't mind riding in back." There was no rhyme or reason for his actions. From somewhere down deep, he didn't want the deputy to have the image of her riding in the cage back there. Chalk it up to Tiernan's chivalry or those pesky protective instincts, but he knew she wasn't a suspect.

"Thank you," Melody said with a grateful look in her eyes as she rounded the front of the SUV and then climbed in the seat. He shut the door behind her and took his place in back.

"Don't let him forget me back here," he said with a slight smile as Calhoun examined the outside of her vehicle, bending down long enough to get a good look at her tires.

"That's a promise," she said. The honesty and determination in those three words shouldn't cause his chest to squeeze.

Which was probably why he felt compelled to add, "No one would blame you for hiring an attorney."

He glanced up at the recording device that was pointed toward Calhoun as he performed his inspection. The audio would reveal what Tiernan had just said but he'd kept the advice generic enough. No one should get too wound up over his words and he'd done nothing wrong.

"Can I ask how you're attached to all of this?"

she asked as she craned her neck around. Her heart-shaped face with those golden eyes made her even more beautiful up close. Her kissable pink lips weren't something he should be focusing on right now, so he managed to force his gaze away.

Since the camera faced the opposite direction, he brought his index finger up to his lips as he fixed his gaze on the recording device. And then he willed her to understand what his actions meant.

MELODY GOT IT. The handsome cowboy in the back seat pointed toward some kind of ceiling-mounted recording device. He didn't want to talk because of the piece of technology spying on them. This man would be called gorgeous by most standards, but she didn't care about his looks right now even though he had the whole tall, muscled, almost intimidatingly handsome bit down to a tee. Since he'd been riding in front, she highly doubted he was a suspect. Who was he and how was he connected to any of this?

Deputy Calhoun climbed into the driver's seat, took a second to acknowledge the musical chairs and then shrugged before closing the door and pulling out of her apartment complex. The passenger in the back seat remained silent. Based on the fact neither seemed to want their conversation replayed in a courtroom someday now that she was on board with the situation, they both stayed quiet on the drive to the sheriff's office.

Melody hoped her questions about the man with cobalt blue eyes would be answered soon. He appeared to have her best interest at heart and yet she had no idea how or why. Patience wasn't exactly her strong suit. With no other choice, she sat back in her seat and recounted the day's events. She'd gotten up early to get ready for her interview and showed up fifteen minutes before her scheduled time. In her mind, not getting the job wasn't an option. She'd pulled out all her tricks in order to put her best foot forward.

Her mind snapped back to how small her problems seemed in comparison with someone being murdered. If she hadn't just spoken to Coop on the phone, she would have been beyond scared for him. He was safe. Her thoughts shifted to her mother.

"Is the person murdered one of my family members?" she asked, breaking the code of silence out of a sense of urgency.

"I don't have a name," Deputy Calhoun stated.

"Male or female?" she quickly followed up. Melody might not be close with her mother but that didn't mean she wouldn't be heartsick if something happened to Tilly Cantor.

The deputy clamped his mouth closed like he was bound by oath not to reveal the sex of the victim.

"I need to know if my mother is alive," she said quietly.

"Male," came the voice from the back seat, a voice that sent a wave of calm along with tingling sensations through her.

The deputy shot a murderous look toward the back.

"I haven't checked my m-a-i-l," the man said with a shrug, trying to cover for the fact he'd just answered a question the lawman didn't. "But I didn't mean to say that out loud."

"I hope you don't feel the need to blurt out any other details, Mr. Hayes," the deputy chastised. It didn't seem to affect the man in the back seat one way or another.

Melody recognized the last name Hayes from Hayes Cattle, one of the most successful ranches in the state. Also, one of the wealthiest families. She should know. The Cantor name used to mix and mingle with only the best. Although, her father had groaned about the Hayes sticking to themselves and not accepting invites. What had he called them? Rich rednecks? The snub had hurt his feelings more than he wanted to admit. But then her dad had always been about social standing over substance.

Given her present circumstance, she wondered if she should heed the handsome stranger's advice and stop talking without a lawyer present. The thought caused a shiver to rock her body. The note was all that much more chilling now that she knew a murder had occurred. Once again, she wondered if someone was trying to lure her out of town and away from civilization. Have her show up to a place that couldn't be traced to a text. The note could have easily been destroyed with a match. The flimsy paper would light up in a heartbeat, leaving no trace it had ever existed. It would look like she'd taken a drive and then never came back.

Would the person have done away with Melody's Camry? Sold it for parts? She'd read the car's popularity made it an easy target for thieves.

Deputy Calhoun pulled into the parking lot of the sheriff's office. There was a jail behind a small brick building. Would she end up behind bars before the day was over? Share a cell with her father?

Tamping down what she hoped was an overreaction, she hopped out of the passenger seat almost as soon as the deputy pulled into a spot. He hadn't cut off the engine before she was opening the back door.

"Tiernan Hayes," he said with a gravelly

campfire voice that awakened parts of her she'd become a little too good at ignoring. As he exited the vehicle, the scent of vapor rub assaulted her. It might be December but the smell caught her off guard. Shouldn't he be wearing Axe or some chick-magnet cologne instead?

Filing the question under *to be continued*, she took the extended hand and shook. A jolt of electricity shot up her arm.

"You already know my name, but I'm Melody Cantor." She wasn't sure why she felt the need for a proper introduction, except that she did. Was it a restart?

"Good to meet you," he said before adding, "Wish it was under better circumstances."

She nodded before wrinkling her nose.

"Are you feeling okay?" she asked. Her grandmother had used swaths of vapor rub whenever Melody had the slightest cough.

"Yes. What makes you ask?" He studied her and her heart practically melted under the scrutiny. Then, he must have caught on because he leaned toward her and whispered, "Helps get rid of the smell of death."

Melody suppressed a gasp. It clicked. He must have found the body.

Chapter Three

Tiernan resisted the urge to drop his hand to the small of Melody's back as he walked her inside. She'd become too quiet after his revelation, no doubt the shock of it all catching up to her. He'd witnessed plenty of dead animals in his day growing up on the ranch, but a human was different. Awful. Tiernan Tough had been a chant from the crowd during his rodeo days. Right now, he felt anything but. The vapor rub had covered up a good part of the scent. But he'd probably never forget it.

The sheriff greeted them in the lobby. He was tall and lanky, wearing all desert brown colors except for a black Stetson, which was appropriate for this time of year. White was reserved for summer.

"Sheriff Cleve Tanner here," he said, extending a handshake to Melody first and then Tiernan, who introduced themselves in turn. "Would you mind waiting in my office while I speak to my deputy?"

Tiernan's gaze shifted to Melody, waiting for the okay. She gave a slight nod.

"Sounds good, Sheriff," Tiernan said before being led down a short hallway and then into an office that looked like a time capsule from the '70s.

"Make yourselves comfortable," Sheriff Tanner instructed, motioning toward the pair of chairs opposite his massive desk. The room was dark with wood paneling lining the walls. The windows were small. There was an American flag and a Texas flag behind and to either side of the cowhide executive chair behind the oak desk.

The sheriff closed the door as he left.

Melody immediately turned to him and grabbed his forearm. "Please tell me what is going on."

Physical contact sent a zing racing up his arm. She seemed to feel something in the same neighborhood, considering she released her grip at the exact moment the zing occurred. She stared at her hands before fisting them and dropping them to her sides.

"I don't know much," he warned, not wanting to get her hopes up too much. "There was a shallow grave on my property. My dog ran after a squirrel and then must have caught a scent. I found him digging at the site. I'd smelled dead animals before and knew the stench didn't come from one of those, so I called 911 rather than disturb the area in case it turned out to be a crime scene."

"How did you know to do all that?" she asked as an eyebrow shot up. "I probably would have trampled all over the place."

"I grew up on a cattle ranch, and have tracked poachers in the past," he said by way of explanation. "The sheriff and his deputies trained us not to disturb a possible crime scene. You'd be surprised at how much information they can get from a shoe print sometimes." His answer resonated, considering she nodded and then took the couple of steps to the pair of chairs. She perched on the nearest one, back ramrod straight. She looked ready to bolt at a moment's notice and like she needed to be as close to the door as possible.

"You already said the...*it* was...a man's body when the deputy refused to discuss the murder," she restated.

"That's right."

"When he first told me the crime was murder, I was worried that it was my mother," she said, twisting her fingers together.

"There any reason your mind went there?" he asked.

"My father is in jail, so it couldn't possibly be him," she said, like she'd just explained her father had gone out for milk.

"When was he arrested and what were the charges?" he asked, figuring this might be an open-and-shut case after all. A father in jail. A piece of paper with her name and address on it. How much danger was she in? Someone could either be trying to locate her or target her.

"Business related," she said before asking, "How are you associated with this crime?"

"The body was found on my property," he explained.

She took in a deep breath before nodding.

"He scammed a lot of people out of money," she continued. "My father, that is."

"Revenge is a good reason to go after someone. Were you somehow connected to your father's business?" he asked.

She shook her head.

"What did the note left on your car say?" he asked, remembering that she'd said something about it to Deputy Calhoun. "The one Calhoun took for evidence."

"It told me to go fifty miles west." Her face twisted in the same confusion he felt.

"That's it? There was no reason given." What were the chances those two events could be coincidental? He doubted it, even though they didn't seem connected on the surface, either. The body had been buried at least a day or two ago. Did the murderer have a plan to get her out of town, knowing there would be heat? Wouldn't the person think to check the victim's pockets? The chances the killing was a random occurrence that was not connected to Melody in some way seemed slim to none. Unless the address was a trail the killer wanted the law to follow.

"No other words were written," she said. "If I was supposed to figure out some hidden meaning behind the message, then I failed miserably."

"We could try rearranging the letters later," he offered.

She gave him a look that said they were two strangers thrown together by circumstance and there would be no later. And then the gravity of the situation dawned on her as she bit down on her bottom lip and pleaded with her eyes.

"Your name was on a piece of paper along with an address in the dead man's front pocket," he finally explained. She deserved to know what she might be up against. The lawmen weren't showing their hand, so to speak.

"That's awful," she said, but recognition dawned. "And that's why Deputy Calhoun came to ask me questions."

"He was checking out your vehicle, as well," he pointed out.

"Which means he was assessing whether or not I was a witness, accomplice or a suspect," she surmised.

"My thoughts exactly," he confirmed. "But I'd like to add a possibility. You could have been the victim's target, and someone stopped him before he got to you."

Melody sucked in a breath.

"I'm just trying to cover all the bases," he quickly added.

She nodded but didn't speak.

"The investigation should reveal how long the victim has been…" He checked her gaze and realized she was still in shock and didn't need a recap of what had happened. "The deputy and sheriff will be able to put together a timeline. It might be a good idea for you to start thinking about how you can prove where you were and maybe think about your own safety when you leave here."

She nodded as some of the spark returned to her eyes. The truth was that she didn't have a whole lot of time to figure out her next moves if this office decided to put her on the suspect list. At this point, Tiernan couldn't say one way or another what the sheriff had up his sleeve. Catching her unaware wasn't something Tiernan could stand by and watch if he had the power to help, especially when she turned those honey-brown eyes on him like she did just now.

"Why are you helping me?" she asked with a lost quality to her voice. The sound was the equivalent of a knife stab to the chest.

"Because I can and it's the right thing to do," he admitted. It was the truth. No one would accuse him of being perfect, but he would never turn his back on someone who needed help.

"You seem to have caught on to something law enforcement hasn't put together yet. What is it?" she continued after a quick nod.

"I just don't see you dragging a body from the trunk of your car to the spot where it was buried. The victim would have had to walk there himself and then climb in the grave," he stated as honestly as he could. Plus, her vulnerability tugged at his heart. She'd seemed genuinely caught off guard when they'd cornered her in her parking spot. Ever since, she'd had that lost quality that he was unable to ignore.

"Do you recognize my last name?" she asked with a raised eyebrow.

He had to think about that one. *Cantor.*

Realization dawned. He remembered reading the reports now. Dots were connecting as to who she was and why she might be defensive around law enforcement. Her father claimed to be innocent of all charges, but the evidence against him was significant and there was a long line of victims who'd lost their life savings.

"You do know who I am," she said with disappointment in her voice.

He confirmed with a nod.

"Is that why you believe you're being treated this way?" he asked.

"Makes sense, doesn't it?" she said without a whole lot of enthusiasm in her voice. "I'm related to Henry Cantor. Therefore, I must be bad, too."

"People aren't their families," he retorted, indignation rising up. He should know, considering he was nothing like Duncan Hayes. That was a story for a whole other time.

"Try convincing other people when their minds are made up," she said with the kind of honesty that left no room for doubt. It was true, though. A family name like theirs came with expectations. Some good, some bad. It all depended on what the others before them had done. In his case, Duncan's reputation in the community was untarnished. At home, he'd been one mean son of a bitch. Insiders knew the man cared more about keeping up appearances than taking care of his own.

"It shouldn't be true," he said on a frustrated sigh.

"But it is," she continued. She was right. The sheriff's next steps would tell them where she stood, and he feared this situation was about to go south for reasons that weren't her fault.

THE DOOR OPENED and then the sheriff walked in. He didn't give off the vibe of being the brightest bulb in the bunch, which worried her. His jaw was slack, and there was a dull quality to his eyes. Sheriff was an elected position and stellar intelligence and qualifications weren't always top of the list with voters. Sometimes, it came down to loyalty and connections to prominent families. She should know. Her father had pulled together plenty of parties over the years with elected officials.

Cleve Tanner's face was scrunched with determination as he walked with a long stride straight to his chair without glancing over. Melody took it as a bad sign. Her heart sank to her toes along with any hope things weren't about to get worse.

"Will you excuse me?" Tiernan said as the sheriff took his seat.

"Uh, I guess so," Sheriff Tanner said, looking up with surprise. Tiernan had caught the man off guard.

"Thank you, sir," Tiernan said. She took note of the formal quality to his voice. He turned to her. "Don't answer any questions until your lawyer arrives. Okay?"

Melody blinked up at Tiernan. He winked just

out of view of the sheriff as if to say *trust me.* Trust was a hard sell for Melody these days. Her belief had been, *I'll trust a person about as far as I can throw them.* For so long, the saying had become ingrained in her. In this case—and mainly because her back was against the wall— she would choose to trust Tiernan.

"Got it," she said to him.

"Cooperating with us now is in your best interest, Ms. Cantor," Sheriff Tanner made a point to say. "You might be able to provide information that could keep the trail of a killer from growing cold."

A couple of responses came to mind. Melody clamped her mouth shut.

"Blame me if anything goes wrong," Tiernan said. "I'm the one advising her not to speak up on behalf of her innocence."

"Hold on there a minute, tiger," Sheriff Tanner said. The man didn't seem to realize just how condescending his tone came across. "No one said she was a suspect. This is an ongoing murder investigation. Time is of the essence."

Tiernan's blue eyes registered the slight. He stood tall and stuffed his hands inside the pockets of his jeans. "Let's be honest, Sheriff. This *is* an ongoing murder investigation, and let's get real about how I've been treated versus how Ms. Cantor has. The body was found on my property, after all. I have a vested interest in finding the real killer and not wasting valuable time and resources."

"You were the one who called it in," Sheriff Tanner pointed out. "I'm aware of the location of the crime scene."

"No one checked my trunk for signs of a struggle or drops of blood," he said. "I'm strong enough to carry dead weight from my vehicle to the spot in question. Why not consider me a suspect? Don't I make a whole lot more sense?"

"You're missing an important point. Your name wasn't found on a slip of paper inside a dead man's pocket," Sheriff Tanner pointed out.

Melody realized Tiernan's genius after the sheriff spoke. He'd just given away his position as to whether or not she was a suspect *and* handed his piece of key evidence over in the process. She had to give it to Tiernan. He was smart. And, based on the sheriff's response, she was in serious trouble. The kind of trouble that involved lawyers and court dates and the possibility of her being handcuffed.

Tiernan fished out his cell phone and held it up. Then, he stepped into the hallway, leaving the door open. From where he stood, she could hear the conversation play out. The lawyer's name he mentioned caused the sheriff to sit up a little straighter. The conversation was short and efficient. The sheriff's gaze narrowed as Tiernan returned to the room.

He held the phone out to Melody.

"All you have to do is agree to representation. John Prescott is on the line," he said to her.

There was no way she could afford to pay him, but she could figure out how to let the attorney down later. Right now, she needed to get the sheriff off her back, so she took the offering.

"Mr. Prescott, this is Melody," she said. Tiernan had already explained to him who she was.

"I'd like to take your case pro bono," Mr. Prescott said. "And, please, call me John."

Several questions popped into her mind along with the saying, *don't look a gift horse in the mouth.*

"I would very much like to be your client, John," she said, making eye contact with a dejected-looking sheriff. She had no idea why Texas's most respected criminal attorney had just offered to work with her, but she had Tiernan Hayes to thank for it. The last name had pull in this state and she would do good to remember the fact. She stopped short of comparing him to her father. Tiernan had on simple clothes—jeans and boots. His calm, polite demeanor was the opposite of her father's charismatic personality. He'd charmed plenty of people out of their money.

"Good," he said. "Would you mind handing the phone to Sheriff Tanner?"

"Not at all." She studied the sheriff. "John would like to speak to you."

"Are you sure this is the path you want to take?" Sheriff Tanner asked as he stared at the phone being offered.

"You haven't given me much of a choice, have you?" she asked.

"Okay, then," Sheriff Tanner said, reaching across the desk for the cell. He held it to his ear. "Yes, sir." There was a beat of silence. "No, sir." Another beat of silence passed. "Well, sir, there's..." John must have cut Tanner off. He brought his other hand up to rub his chin. "She's right here."

The phone came back over the massive desk as Sheriff Tanner rested his elbows on his desk in a look of defeat.

"This is Melody again," she said.

"Tanner should be telling you that he doesn't have any further questions," John said. "I'm sending a car to pick you and Tiernan up. I'd like to meet as soon as possible, and since you're closer to Tiernan's house, I thought that might be faster. Can I tell the driver to take you home with Tiernan?"

"I guess that would be okay," she said, figuring a change of clothes would have to wait. There was no way she could go back to the office today. Everything was happening fast, and she needed a minute to process. It would probably be good to have a conversation with Tiernan, considering the body had been found on his property. He'd given her a quick rundown a few minutes ago. The information was beginning to take seed and questions were taking shape. Or maybe she just needed to hear it all again, slower this time. A man was dead who had her name and address in his pocket. She wouldn't rest until she figured out who he was and why he was trying to find her.

"Good," John said. "Do you mind giving the phone back to Tiernan?"

"No, not at all," she said. "Thank you for taking this case."

"Innocent people deserve good representation," John said with conviction that made her believe he was the best person for the job.

She thanked him again before handing the phone over to Tiernan. Their fingers grazed and she did her best to hide the sensual shiver that ran up her arm. More of that warmth exploded in her chest as their gazes locked.

Melody took in a breath, trying to calm her nerves. The vapor rub scent was a stark reminder

of the real reason she was in the same room with
Tiernan Hayes. A man who might have been
coming after her had been murdered. And she
would do whatever it took to find out why she'd
just become a target.

Chapter Four

"We'll be leaving now, Sheriff," Tiernan said, as he leaned against the doorjamb after closing out the call with the hotshot lawyer who was on board to represent Melody. "Unless you have any additional questions, in which case I'll get Prescott back on the line."

Sheriff Tanner shifted his gaze to a spot in the corner of the room where the ceiling met two walls. He picked up a pencil on his desk, broke it in half and said, "I guess we're done here. But Ms. Cantor is advised not to leave town without contacting my office first."

"Her phone works anywhere, so unless you have a reason to detain her here, she can go anywhere she pleases," Tiernan continued, not liking the sheriff's reactions.

"Free country," Tanner conceded with a frown as he tossed the splintered wooden pieces on top of his desk.

Melody walked out of the office and into the

hallway, whispering a thank-you as she passed by. Tiernan held back the urge to smile. First of all, it was way too early to claim victory with the sheriff. He might not come off as the most intelligent person, but it was anyone's guess who might be behind the man, pulling the strings. The sheriff had to have connections in order to get the job in the first place, which meant he could be tied to prominent families—families who weren't too thrilled with the daughter of Henry Cantor. Greed was right up there on the list of motives for murder.

Melody stood beside him in the parking lot. She rubbed her arms to stave off the sudden chill in the air. Tiernan had to resist the urge to wrap his arm around her to keep her warm.

A dark blue SUV arrived within ten minutes at almost the same second Prescott texted the ride should be pulling up. Tiernan acknowledged the driver with a nod before opening the door to the middle row of seats. He offered a hand to help Melody climb inside. His reaction to skin on skin contact as she took the offering left him speechless. He climbed in behind her, clearing his throat to ease some of the sudden dryness. He hadn't had this type of reaction to touching someone in longer than he cared to remember.

After closing the door behind him, he turned

his attention to the driver as Melody buckled in. "I'm guessing you already have my address."

"Yes, sir," he said. "We are good to go."

The ride to Tiernan's house was quiet. He didn't expect much talking in the presence of the driver, but he could also see the wheels turning in Melody's mind. Tiernan wasn't too far off from spinning out mentally, considering his thoughts kept looping back to the body found on his property. Loki was home alone, too. The Lab mix had no idea he'd uncovered a dead body—lucky him. Still, Tiernan had been away for hours. Loki needed to go out. He needed attention.

The driver stopped in front of Tiernan's porch. After thanking him for the ride home, Tiernan slipped out of his side and came around the back of the vehicle to open the door for Melody. Once again, sparks flew when she took his hand as she climbed down. She suppressed a yawn for the third time in ten minutes. All the adrenaline from the day would be wearing thin by now.

After Tiernan closed the door, the driver pulled away. Tiernan reached for Melody's hand and then linked their fingers. As soon as he unlocked the door to his home—using a key to enter was something he'd never done before—he stepped beside Melody to intercept an overenthusiastic Loki. At one year old, the rescue dog still had more puppy energy than brain development to stop his impulses. The ball of excitement and energy barreled toward them from his spot by the sliding glass doors across the room in the dining area. The main living area was open concept. He didn't need a whole lot of privacy considering he lived alone.

Tiernan dropped Melody's hand and stepped in front of her to shield her from Loki. When her hands came up to his back, her nails dug into his shoulders and she hunkered down behind him, he realized she was afraid.

"I probably should have warned you about this guy, but he doesn't have an aggressive bone in his body," he reassured as Loki put on the brakes and skidded toward them on the rug. His big paws got away from him, as usual, causing him to bowling ball slide into Tiernan's shins.

"It's fine," she said with a tone that said anything but. Tiernan had learned the hard way those two words strung together oftentimes meant the opposite.

He bent down and scratched Loki's belly. Melody backed into the corner. His heart went out to her.

"Go ahead and make yourself comfortable," he said to her before leading the Lab outside by the collar.

Loki did his business almost immediately.

Accidents inside the house had been few and far between in recent months. Tiernan picked up a tennis ball from the basket on the small porch, and then threw it. He repeated the game long enough for Loki to burn off some of his energy—energy that was never in short supply with the breed.

By the time he walked inside again, Melody was perched on a bar stool at the granite island in his kitchen. Muscles corded, breathing shallow, she looked ready to jump at the slightest noise. She white-knuckled the wooden stool as Loki bolted toward her.

"Loki, sit," Tiernan said in a calm but direct voice. To his surprise, Loki did. After running out Loki's energy, it was about a fifty-fifty shot as to whether the dog would listen. "Behave."

"I got bit as a kid, so big dogs still scare me even though I know all dogs aren't like my neighbor's," Melody confessed.

"I'm sorry that happened. Loki's energy can be over the top," he responded. "But I can assure you that he would never bite, not even playfully."

She nodded, her gaze still locked on to the dog. When someone had a bad experience early on with an animal, trying to convince them not all dogs were out of control was useless. Tiernan hoped she would stick around long enough to see that Loki wasn't a threat, and maybe change her mind about animals. Or at the very least plant a seed. Loki might be a hot mess at times but Tiernan couldn't imagine his life without him.

"Give me a sec to get him squared away," he said to her as he crossed the room toward the pantry where he kept dry food.

"Do whatever you need to," she said.

Tiernan filled the dog's bowl and then topped it off with half a can of wet food. "Steak and rice today, buddy."

"How old is...*he*...right?" Melody asked. "He's a boy." There wasn't a whole mess of confidence in her tone about Loki's sex.

"Yes. He's a boy," Tiernan confirmed. Loki had already hopped up and resumed his position as Tiernan's shadow. "The shelter where Loki came from found him digging through the trash at a construction site, searching for food."

Her face twisted in a grimace. "Poor baby."

"He'd been underweight as a three-month-old, but they got him in time before he was completely malnourished," he continued.

"Do they know where he spent those early months?" she asked.

He shrugged. "It's anyone's guess according to the volunteer. There were no others like him found in the area. No lactating mother anywhere, either."

"Sounds like someone might have abandoned

him after taking him away from his family," she said as some of the tension lines eased in her forehead and the corners of her mouth curled into a frown. An emotion passed behind her eyes as she glanced over at Loki, a mix of compassion and heartbreak. "I've heard of people driving out to the country to drop off puppies or dogs they no longer want."

Tiernan gritted his teeth before nodding.

"He was flea bitten and scared, but his heart was still open to learning and trusting. Many more weeks in the old environment fending for himself could easily have changed that," he explained. "Which would have been a shame because his heart is as big as the Texas sky."

"It's surprisingly easy to become so broken by life that you can't ever get back to that innocent trust again," Melody said before compressing her lips like she'd just given away more than she probably should with the statement.

"All I know is the minute those big brown eyes looked up at me from behind the plexiglass, I knew I'd found my next best friend," he said. "No more dumpster diving for this guy. Only the best. A comfortable place to lay his head down every night and someone who will make sure he never suffers again."

"He's lucky to have you," Melody said with a small crack in her voice that caused him to wonder about her background. A sound like the one she'd just made came with a backstory, one he hoped she'd stick around long enough to tell him.

LOKI MIGHT BE a tornado but his story softened Melody toward the hyped-up animal. When she really looked at him, she found the warmest pair of brown eyes. It would be impossible to be scared of the Lab after knowing what he'd been through in those formative months. Even after living with Tiernan for some time, Loki still inhaled his food. Was that because of his past? Was it something he could ever get over? Or would he always eat fast for fear the meal would be taken away?

Melody didn't grow up with dogs, so she had no idea what they thought or needed. A couple of her friends had owned tiny dogs that could fit inside a purse. Loki had to be in the seventy-five-to one-hundred-pound range. He was definitely goofy, she decided as she watched him slop water all over the floor around his bowls. When she really thought about it, he did have more of a "big kid" energy than fierce beast.

With a sigh, she decided that she actually felt sorry enough for him to be brave the next time he came barreling toward her or bolting past so fast he accidently crashed into her legs.

Tiernan walked over to the fridge, and she forced her gaze away from his muscled backside. He had the kind of broad shoulders that were far too tempting to look at for long. Her body's reaction reminded her just how long it had been since she'd had good sex...any sex. Her thoughts were bouncing all over the place. Anything to avoid thinking about the fact a person was dead and had been buried in a shallow grave on this man's property. If that wasn't horrific enough, her name was somehow connected.

It was awful.

"I have enough leftovers to feed us both," Tiernan's voice broke through. "If you don't mind pasta."

"Pasta's good," she said, figuring she wouldn't be able to eat much anyway.

"Then, I have spaghetti from a restaurant and a mean lasagna that I made on my own," he said without looking back.

"You cook?" The question came out faster and sounding more shocked than she meant it to. "Wait, that wasn't what I intended to say."

He spun around with a disgusted look on his face that almost made her laugh.

"You don't think men can cook?" he asked with more of that disdain coming through.

She put her hands up in the air, palms out, in

the surrender position. "I heard how it sounded the minute it came out of my mouth. I just didn't think you would know how to make Italian food. Most guys are more on-the-grill types in my experience."

"All I can say to that is maybe you've been around the wrong people," he said as he cracked a smile. "You're taking the lasagna because now I have something to prove."

"I was going to ask for it anyway," she teased, appreciating a precious few moments of levity. She had a feeling the lawyer from the phone call would be here soon and all lightness would be sucked out of the room when they went through the details of everything they knew so far about the case.

Loki stood at the pair of sliding glass doors, looking anxious.

"Should I let him out again while you heat up food?" she asked, surprising herself with the question.

"Never hurts," he said with the kind of ease that made her feel at home.

Tiernan's hospitality was most likely ingrained in him, given his background as a Hayes, but there was something special about his calm demeanor that she reminded herself not to get used to. Pretty soon, she would be walking right out the front door and heading back to her apartment. Alone.

The thought of being by herself tonight sent an icy chill racing up her spine. She stood up and then walked over to the glass doors, first unlocking and then sliding one side open. Loki glanced up at her with those brown eyes and her heart melted a little more.

"Go on," she said for lack of anything better. She had no idea how to tell a dog to go outside.

Loki obeyed and a trill of satisfaction coursed through her. The biting incident happened when she was in kindergarten. Maybe it was time to let it go.

"Should I follow him outside?" she asked.

"He knows what to do," he said as a buzzer dinged and the smell of Italian filled the air. "Leave the door cracked and he'll come in when he's ready."

"Sounds like a plan," she said, turning around to the sight of Tiernan setting a plate down where she'd been sitting. "I doubt I can eat much."

"Try. For me," he said in a gentle way that caused her to sit down and pick up her fork. He had the kind of masculine voice that had a way of rolling over her and through her. "Besides, Prescott will be here soon and we'll go over the details of everything that happened when he arrives. For now, we have a few more moments of peace and quiet."

The dread in his voice connected on a soul level with the emotions running wild through her. It was next to impossible not to think about what had happened or who might be involved. And yet, the idea of getting a break even for a little while sounded too good to be true.

"Okay," she said on a soft sigh. When did life become so complicated? Unsure she could get down one bite despite the amazing smell of the lasagna, she surprised herself in cleaning her plate.

"I take it you approve?" Tiernan said with a smirk that caused her heart to flip.

"It wasn't awful," she teased back.

He picked up her plate and stacked it on top of his. "Good to know that I rank right up there a notch above awful." When he made eye contact, her heart skipped another beat. The man was good-looking, to say the least. The fact he could cook put him in a whole new category of great catch. So much so, she glanced around for signs of female companionship. There was no way this man was unattached. Melody bit down on her bottom lip rather than ask his relationship status. Besides, it was none of her business and she was clearly hanging on to topics that would help her avoid thinking about the tragic—and possibly dangerous—current circumstances she found herself in.

"We both know the lasagna was mouthwateringly good," she said. "I just didn't think you were the kind of person who needed the ego boost with a whole bunch of flattery."

"When it comes to cooking, my ego can use all the help it can get," he said as he ran the dishes underneath the water in the sink.

"Well, it was amazing," she reassured. "And I'm the one who should be doing the dishes since you cooked."

"Reheated," he countered. "There's a difference." He didn't miss a beat. "And thank you for the compliment."

"You cooked my meal at some point," she said with a fist on her hip. Negotiating with this man didn't seem like it was going to do her a whole lot of good.

The sound of tires pulling up the drive stopped all light conversation. It was like a heavy cloud descended over the room, the air suddenly thick. She needed to know the details of what was going on despite nothing inside her wanting to hear specifics on how a man was murdered. Then there was the lawyer who was now her defense attorney. She would be pressed to go into the whole story behind her father's incarceration.

Dredging up the past was the worst. She avoided talking about her family at all costs. Now, she had no choice. Moving to the kitchen window, she watched a polished-looking man exit his Suburban. The serious look on his face fired off warning shots as she tried to prepare for what was ahead.

Chapter Five

John Prescott was several inches shorter than Tiernan's six-foot-three-inch height. He was slim with a runner's build and someone who probably played tennis on the weekends with his wife at the country club. He'd graduated UT Law first in his class and had a national reputation for winning in court. Tiernan hoped bringing in Prescott for Melody's case was overkill, but he wouldn't take any chances considering she was being treated as a suspect instead of a witness.

Tiernan moved to the front door and then opened it before Prescott reached the small porch. "Thank you for coming and taking this case personally." The man, the legend of Texas law, wouldn't normally handle a case that wasn't highly visible but he'd come from Cider Creek, just like Tiernan, and folks from there had a way of sticking together. Their families knew each other and went way back. Prescott was a few years older than Tiernan, so the two had never been in the same grade in school.

"No question," Prescott said without hesitation. He hopped the couple of steps onto the porch, and then extended a hand. A small laptop was tucked underneath his left arm. His grayish-blue slacks were tailored, as was his steel-colored shirt. His handshake was firm and relayed a message of confidence. His gaze shifted over Tiernan's right shoulder to Melody, who was standing behind him. Tiernan could feel her presence without looking back.

"Mr. Prescott," she said. Her voice had a forced calm that said she was anything but. He could only imagine what must be going through her mind right now.

"Please, call me John," Prescott said as Tiernan stepped aside so the two could shake hands.

"Melody," she said in response.

"Come in," Tiernan urged as Loki plodded over. The full stomach helped calm his two-year-old-after-eating-a-bowl-of-candy demeanor. Night was always the best time with him after he'd played out most of his energy. He had two speeds, breakneck pace and dead stop. In the evenings, Loki would curl up on the couch next to Tiernan while he watched a game.

Tiernan led them into the kitchen as Loki loped along, straggling and bringing up the rear.

"Does anyone want coffee?" he asked.

Prescott looked to Melody. She nodded. "Make it three," he said.

"Won't take but a second," Tiernan said, moving into the kitchen and quickly putting on a pot. He'd always been one of those people who could drink a cup and still fall asleep an hour later.

"Who is this, by the way?" Prescott set his laptop down on the granite island and then took a knee beside Loki, whose tail was cranking up to a feverish wag. It was a good indicator of his energy level. The attention pushed him into hyper mode.

"That would be Loki," Tiernan said. The dog rolled over onto his back, exposing his belly in a display of complete trust. Prescott had a way with animals that impressed Tiernan.

"He's a good boy," Prescott said. Anyone who was this good with dogs couldn't be a bad person. It had become a litmus test of sorts and held true to this day. Tiernan kept an eye on anyone a good dog didn't take to.

After a few minutes of tummy scratching, mugs were filled with coffee. Tiernan brought them over and set them down as Prescott stood up then took an empty stool. He sat farthest to the left, Melody took the middle seat and Tiernan sat to her right. She pushed her chair away from the granite island far enough for everyone to be able to see each other's faces before picking up her coffee mug and rolling it around in her palms. A nervous tick?

The ease from earlier was gone. Tension so thick Tiernan could cut it with a knife filled the room as Prescott opened his laptop and booted up.

"The reason it took me a while to get here is because I drove past your house on the way," Prescott stated with a frown. He grabbed the cup by the rim and managed a sip before setting it down again. "I crossed paths with the sheriff and a deputy who were on your street."

"What? Why would they be at my home?" she asked as concern lines wrinkled her forehead. Tiernan wondered the same thing. Why?

"It's not unexpected in a murder case," Prescott said, stopping long enough to turn and make eye contact with Melody. "But it says they are looking at you as a suspect, so we need to keep our guards up at this point."

"Are they planning to arrest me?" she asked.

"Not today, they're not," he said. "I intend to keep it that way."

"How?" she asked, a slight tremor in her voice.

"By proving your innocence, for one. I have investigators on the case to make sure the law dots every *i* and crosses every *t*. They'll do their jobs correctly and find the real suspect. My people will also be searching for a killer," he continued.

Melody nodded but there was pure panic in her eyes.

"My father is…"

"I know about Henry Cantor," Prescott said with sympathy. "You aren't your father, but we will be battling against his reputation."

Melody sucked in a breath. "Just when I think I can distance myself from my father, something like this would happen, linking me with his name again and dragging me down right with him."

"I'm sorry to ask this, given what sounds like a difficult relationship with your father. I know all the information that has been in the news about him so far. What else do I need to know? I'll need you to tell me about everything."

"Can I ask why you're locking on to my father?" she asked, cocking her head to one side.

"The description of the person who was killed matched up with a missing-person's report. Nothing has been ID'd, or should I say released, about the deceased but I have someone on the inside at the coroner's office." Prescott leaned forward as he spoke. "This is unconfirmed information, so it goes without saying that it doesn't leave this room."

"Okay," Melody said with trepidation in her voice. The kind that said she realized she needed to know what was about to come out of the lawyer's mouth but wasn't all that sure she actually wanted to. Riding the fence meant she didn't fall onto either side. It meant she was still in the in-between state of not knowing the horrific and real details, and having to deal with the news. Not exactly bliss but not hell, either.

"You know I won't say anything," Tiernan reassured when Prescott's gaze shifted to him.

"The victim was bludgeoned to death with a sharp object, possibly an axe," Prescott began as Melody shuttered.

"Sorry for the directness," Prescott said.

Melody took in a slow breath. "I need to hear this. Please. Go on."

"Based on lividity, he was killed forty-eight hours ago. His name is Jason Riker," Prescott said, then not so subtly checked Melody's reaction. "Does that name ring any bells?"

"Not for me, it doesn't," she said. "I feel like it should, though."

She told him about the note she found on her vehicle after the job interview.

"Do you have an approximate time the note was left?" Prescott asked as he turned toward the small laptop and then opened a file. He made a note of the incident.

"My interview was at nine thirty sharp," she said. "I was there for about an hour. It was there when I got out."

Prescott nodded and added the time and then pulled up a map. "That would put you about…"

"Blanco, Johnson City or Meadowlakes," she said before Prescott could run his finger fifty miles west. The cities had been committed to memory. "What's going to happen at my home? What's happening right now?"

"Right. Sorry. The sheriff called on a judge to issue a search warrant, saying he has an informant," Prescott said.

"They won't find anything," she said almost immediately.

There was a scenario in which she was being set up. Tiernan had no plans to mention his theory at this point. But it meant the sheriff might actually find "evidence" linking her to the crime.

As Melody took a sip of coffee, Tiernan made eye contact with Prescott. The lawyer had the same idea, and there was something else. A piece of information that he was keeping to himself. Based on the look on his face, it was important.

"I have someone checking into any possible connections between you and the victim,"

Prescott said after Melody set her mug down on the hard granite.

Was that it? He'd found a link?

MELODY DIDN'T LIKE the sound of any of this. Her home was being picked through at this very moment and she'd never felt so helpless in all her life. Correction, this was the second time she'd felt completely helpless. The first happened when she caught her father, pants down, growling and grunting in a way that made her nauseous to think about to this day. She mentally shook off the image. And now this. All her private things being examined as her home was searched. This felt like a violation of the worst kind.

Tiernan reached over and took her hand in his as though he sensed she needed the reassurance. His touch brought on a lot of distracting sensations that she couldn't focus on right now.

"I apologize in advance for the next question that I have to ask," Prescott began. "Will the sheriff find anything incriminating in your home?"

Melody shook her head vigorously. "Absolutely not."

"Okay, good," Prescott said. His face was a study in calm whereas Melody was starting to freak out.

Tiernan squeezed her hand and more of that warmth spread through her, bringing her pulse down another notch.

"Tell me about your family," Prescott continued without missing a beat.

"My parents are divorced. Have been for quite some time now," she said. It was strange focusing on the details of her family, considering she spent most of her time trying to avoid the topic altogether while distancing herself from them. "I have a brother by the name of Coop. His actual name is Henry Cooper Cantor III, but we've always called him Coop."

"How well do the two of you get along?" Prescott asked.

The answer to his question was complicated and she hated getting into the details of their family dynamic. Since her freedom might be on the line, she cleared her throat and started. "I used to look up to my brother. He's a few years older than I am and was a shining star in our family. He was athletic and popular in school. He was always nice to me. I was his kid sister. I thought we were this idyllic family. My mom was a tennis mom who had wine nights with the other moms from the small college prep school my brother and I attended."

She stopped long enough to take a sip of coffee.

"My world came crashing down when I

caught my father with my English teacher," she said before compressing her lips into a frown. "My brother defended our father, saying it was just boys being boys."

"It's hard to believe jerks out there still believe that load of crap," Tiernan said low and under his breath. She couldn't agree more.

"Your brother, Coop, is in business with your father, correct?" Prescott asked.

"That's right," she confirmed.

"And yet he hasn't been arrested," Prescott continued, making notes in the computer.

"No. He hasn't," she said. "He maintains our father's innocence."

"The evidence against your father isn't exactly minute," Prescott said, sounding as surprised as she'd been when she'd first heard her brother defending the man.

"According to my brother, our father has done nothing wrong, not in business or in life," she said.

"What do you believe?" Prescott asked.

"He's guilty," she said without hesitation. Saying the words stung. This wasn't what she wanted to believe about her father. There was strong evidence pointing toward his guilt and she knew he cheated in his marriage. It made sense the man would be no different in his business affairs.

"Your brother has a vested interest in your father coming out of this situation with a clear record," Prescott noted. Then came exactly what she'd been thinking. "The feds could come after him next."

"Yes, and they most likely will," she said. "The way he's defending our father makes me fear Coop is covering his own tail, as well. Family loyalty is one thing. His reaction to our conversation recently made me think he might be hiding something, and I'm afraid he's going to end up going down the same path if he hasn't already."

"Your father's arrest could be a wake-up call," Tiernan spoke up. "If he is aboveboard in his dealings and honestly didn't know what your father was doing."

"It's possible our father could have been shielding Coop from what was really going on," she said, appreciating Tiernan's viewpoint. She figured everyone would write her brother off based on his association with the business. She could only hope for his sake that he wasn't up to his eyeballs in it. "My brother would believe anything our father said, take it at face value."

"For now, we'll assume innocent until evidence states otherwise," Prescott said. "It doesn't hurt to keep a close eye on your brother." Those sobering words would keep her up at night.

"You don't think he would commit murder and then implicate me, do you?" she asked, hating to hear those words come out of her mouth. It was awful to be in a position to have to think them let alone say them out loud.

"Right now, I'm considering every possibility," Prescott said with an apologetic look.

One of the worst things about her father destroying their family by cheating was that he never once apologized for his actions.

"Is there an inheritance?" Prescott asked.

"None that I'm aware of," she said, issuing a small sigh. "And I doubt my father would give me anything anyway, after the way I treated my trust fund." The thought of what she'd done was almost enough to make her smile.

"What was that, if I may ask?" Prescott asked.

"Donated it to local-area food banks," she admitted. "It wasn't like I was trying to throw anything in my parents' faces with the gesture, even though they took it that way. My brother flipped out. It's part of the reason none of us are close. I work a regular job with a jerk of a boss, and I live in a small apartment over someone's garage. But when I put my head on the pillow every night, I sleep just fine. I wonder if others in my family can say the same thing."

A cell phone buzzed but no one made an immediate move toward one.

"That's mine," Prescott finally said when it went off again. He pulled a small, thin cell from his front pocket that she didn't even realize was there. As he read the text that had come through, he frowned.

Melody's heart sank to her toes. This news was going to be bad.

Chapter Six

Hearing about Melody donating her trust fund to
feed the hungry caused Tiernan to look at her in
a whole new light. From the sounds of it, she'd
been through the ringer with her family and was
determined to come out the other side stronger
and more independent. Those were traits he ad-
mired in a person. But Prescott's phone and his
expression brought Tiernan's attention back to
the present problem.

"I told you that I have investigators working
on the case in the background," Prescott said.

Melody nodded as Tiernan squeezed her hand.
He wanted her to know she had support because
she'd received precious little. The way a lightning bolt struck the center of his chest when
she squeezed back made him wonder how much
trouble he was in with her.

"Turns out, Jason Riker is your half-brother,"
Prescott said with a grim expression.

Melody sucked in a breath as a look of shock stamped her features.

"Then it's possible he was coming to meet me and not try to kill me," she surmised. He hoped she wasn't being too optimistic. Although, as far as he knew there were no weapons found on the victim. Which didn't mean there weren't any. They could have been taken or used on Jason.

"I probably shouldn't be surprised that I have a half-brother...*had*," she corrected herself, "out there somewhere all these years. Maybe the better question is whether there are more siblings."

"I'll have to see if I can get access to the accounting from your father's arrest. I might be able to gain access to the specific evidence against him. Although, it's still early. Your father has been arrested and the DA will be very careful about not giving away the specifics of his evidence," Prescott said. "Unless I can link these two cases and then the DA's office will have to hand it over while I'm in discovery."

"The thought of connecting my name to my father's during this trial isn't exactly warm and fuzzy," Melody said. "I can also probably kiss off the job I interviewed for, as well. Possibly even my job when news gets out that I'm now linked to a murder and under suspicion." She grabbed her cell phone and fired off a text to say she wasn't coming in.

"I'll do my best to suppress the news, but this will be public record," Prescott warned. "The sheriff shouldn't want information leaking about an ongoing murder investigation. I'd have more confidence in his law enforcement abilities if I felt he got the job on merit."

"I've never had occasion to meet the man before," Tiernan conceded. "My opinion after today is right on target with yours."

Melody nodded.

"Do you have any questions for me?" Prescott asked as he closed his laptop. He turned and gave his full attention to Melody, making eye contact.

"I'm sure I'll have a million by morning," she said, suppressing a yawn. "Right now, I just want to go home and put my head on the pillow in the hopes this was all a bad dream."

"Fair warning," Prescott said. "There may be reporters on your doorstep."

Melody sucked in a breath.

"Why?" She opened her mouth to ask another question and then clamped it shut almost as quickly. "Never mind."

"Is there somewhere else you can stay for a few days until all the attention dies down?" Prescott asked.

"How about here?" Tiernan asked without giving it much thought. "You're here already.

You've yawned three times in the last few minutes. I have a guest room that's sitting there empty."

"It's not a bad idea," Prescott urged. "If I need to get a hold of either of you for additional questions, you'd be together."

Melody took a few moments to mull it over. She finally nodded. "If it's not too much trouble, I'd like to stay tonight."

Prescott stood and then tucked his laptop underneath his arm. "Lay low for a few days if at all possible."

"I can call in sick from work," she said. "If I still have a job."

Prescott nodded and offered a look of sympathy.

"For what it's worth, not many people would care how they got their inheritance," he said. "The fact you did and were willing to walk away from a trust fund because you felt others were defrauded out of money says a lot about your character. It's an honor to defend you."

Melody's smile didn't reach her eyes but it was easy to see she appreciated the words.

"I don't know if it was my smartest move now that I'm likely to be unemployed when I wake up tomorrow," she quipped. "But it still feels like I made the right decision a few years ago, so I wouldn't change a thing."

Prescott's smile was big enough for all three of them. "Ma'am." He nodded toward Tiernan before saying, "I can show myself out."

Tiernan followed anyway so he could lock the door. Melody sat at the granite island, her expression a little lost. Her life had been turned upside down today, and the exhaustion was beginning to show.

"If you want to shower, there are always fresh linens in the bathroom. Soap and shampoo is always stocked," he continued. "There's a bathrobe hanging on the back of the door. You're welcome to use it."

Melody nodded. She glanced around the room. "Where does Loki sleep?"

"Usually out here in the main living room. I leave my door open, and he comes in and out as he pleases," he said.

She glanced over at the couch and then at Loki's bed, where he'd gone to curl up in a ball. "Mind if I sleep out here?"

"On the couch?" he asked, thinking a bed would be far more comfortable for her. And then it dawned on him. Was she scared to sleep alone?

"IF YOU DON'T MIND, I'd rather be out here," Melody answered after a beat of silence. The couch looked comfortable enough and she had no desire to sleep in a strange bed alone. Based on the layout, in the guest room she'd be on the opposite side of the cabin, far away from Tiernan. The irrational fear someone could break in and somehow get to her crept into her thoughts. Now that it was there, it would be impossible to get rid of. Plus, even though she was tired, she wondered if she could get any real sleep anyway.

"Not a problem," Tiernan said. "I have a few things to address on the work front, so I'll be out here while you shower."

"Oh, good," she said. Having him nearby sent another wave of calm through her. She realized her concerns were probably unfounded and yet she couldn't quite shake them off, either. Knowing someone died either coming after her in order to hurt her or searching for her for some kind of answers or connection was wreaking havoc on her mind.

She excused herself after being told where to find the shower. The layout was intuitive and the furnishings comfortable. There was a masculinity to the design, with the oversize leather sofa across from a tumbled stone fireplace. The cabin had large rooms with high ceilings and looked more high-end resort on the inside than fishing cabin.

The rain shower had good pressure and the warm water was heaven on earth. If only she could wash off this day. Melody ended the shower, dried off and slipped on the white cotton robe. She cinched the belt around her waist, pulling it tight to ensure the robe stayed closed. She scooped up her business suit, wishing she had casual clothes with her. She didn't even have her car, not that it would matter. She wasn't leaving town so there were no extra clothes in the back seat. Her gym bag was at home. All she had with her was what she'd put on that morning. Morning seemed so long ago.

"Do you have anything I can put these dirty clothes in?" she asked after clearing her throat. She didn't want to surprise Tiernan as he sat there in one of his oversize leather chairs that flanked the fireplace, gaze intensely focused on the laptop.

He made an immediate move to set the tech down on the floor beside his chair and get up. "I'll take those." He cut across the living room and took the ball of clothes from her hands.

"All I need is a grocery bag or something to put these in until I can swing by my house tomorrow," she said, then realized it might not be so easy to do that if reporters and the law could be snooping around. Murder wasn't something that happened every day in small towns like Mesquite Spring. Austin was another story altogether.

"I'll throw them in the wash," he said as she let go.

"I can do it if you point me in a direction," she said. "Besides, you've already done enough for one day."

"Don't worry about it," he said, like it was nothing. "The washer and dryer are in the hallway leading to my bedroom. I have to head that way to take a shower anyway, so it's no trouble."

"If you're sure," she said.

"I'm good," he confirmed with a small smile.

"I found the toothbrush and supplies in the basket on the counter," she said. "Are you always this prepared for company?" She didn't want to go there in her mind that he had a string of women who came through a revolving front door. The lack of female touches in the home and the fact he didn't wear a gold band reassured her there didn't seem to be anyone special in his life.

He shrugged as his smile grew, revealing perfectly straight, white teeth. "I have a housekeeper who comes in once a week to take care of all those details. I'll be sure to thank her on your behalf when she comes in Monday."

"Thank you," she said. "To both of you." Her gaze dropped down to his Cupid's bow mouth where it lingered. Suddenly, she realized just how naked she was underneath the cotton covering.

Standing this close was a bad idea, so she

took a step back, thankful she didn't fall. She wasn't exactly the athletic one in the family. She left sports up to her brother, who'd played just about everything.

"I put out blankets and a pillow on the couch," Tiernan said. "There's still a few things for work that I need to handle, so I'll grab my laptop when I'm out of the shower. It'll only take me a few minutes. Are you good if I come back in the living room?"

"Of course," she said. "As tired as I am, it'll be hard to shut down my thoughts. I'm just looking forward to lying down for a little while and shutting down as much as possible. You won't bother me if you work in here. In fact, it might be nice to have company in the room."

"Okay," he said. "I'll be back in a few minutes." He exited the room. She was grateful Loki was content to stay with her.

After drinking a full glass of water, she made a bed on the sofa. Her cell was inside her purse, turned off. She'd flipped it off after the meeting with the sheriff on the ride home. As she climbed underneath the cover, she started thinking about all the stuff she needed to take care of. She'd left her boss hanging today and was afraid to check in at this point. They would manage at the office fine without her. It was a real estate development office, not a hospital. Still, work piled up on a daily basis. She could only imagine how many calls and texts were waiting on her phone, not to mention her email. The iPad in her purse was turned off, too. It was probably good for her sanity but not her livelihood. She had a little money saved. It wasn't like she spent money on anything but rent and food. She'd been needing to walk away from her bully of a boss for months. He kept her so busy she didn't have time to look for another job until today. She figured that was by design. The pay was good even though the hours were long. The last straw had been when he'd thought it was perfectly okay for his son to hit on her. The kid wasn't old enough to legally drink. Meanwhile, she was thirty-three years old. The boss had called his college son's actions "harmless." The real estate development company was small and family owned. Her HR contact was a relative of the boss. The only option was to find another job where she would be respected.

This wasn't the time to be angry with herself for not listening to her small circle of friends—friends she'd lost touch with because she'd been too busy to keep up relationships over the past three years. Too many years had been sacrificed with little time off only to end up being chased around a desk like the #metoo movement hadn't happened. Time wasn't stuck in the past, when men got away with bad behavior with a slap on a back and a cigar.

Maybe being forced to quit would end up being a good thing for her. Maybe she shouldn't let it get her down. Maybe this was exactly the push she needed to get a real fire under her backside about getting another job. As soon as the new one read about her in the news, they would rescind their offer—if there was going to be one in the first place.

Thinking about work only depressed her.

Melody shifted her thoughts to what she knew so far about the case. Someone had tried to get her far away from the area at around the time the body was found. Everyone was a suspect and she needed to keep them at arm's length at least for a few days until the news cycle shifted and attention moved to something else. There was always a new, bigger story in Texas these days. Could she outlast the interest?

She fluffed the pillow as a bare-chested Tiernan walked into the room. It dawned on her that she knew very little about the man. Since she figured sleep was about as close as rayon to silk, she decided asking a few questions couldn't hurt.

"Mind if I ask what you do for a living?" she asked, motioning toward the laptop on the floor.

He walked over and sat down as she forced her gaze away from ripples of lean muscle and droplets of water rolling down olive skin. Jeans hung low on his hips. The man was billboard-worthy hotness that had her throat drying up at the sight of him.

"I make custom saddles," he supplied.

"For horses?" she asked, realizing there weren't many other kinds. "Never mind. Stupid question."

"There are no stupid questions," he said with a warm smile that had a way of lowering her defenses while putting her at ease. A sharp contrast to butterflies going wild in her chest every time she looked into those disarmingly blue eyes of his. Dark hair and stunning eyes got her every time.

"What kinds of saddles? Like, for a major chain or feed stores?" she asked.

"Mine are custom," he said with a raised eyebrow. "You really don't know who I am, do you?"

The question got her attention but the amusement in his eyes piqued her interest even more. "Not really. Not personally, despite knowing you have a big last name. Why? Is that bad?"

He laughed. The deep timbre sent a trill of awareness skittering across her skin.

"That's a good thing in my book," he said.

"I'm afraid you're going to have to tell me if

you don't want me to do a Google search later," she said.

"Don't do that," he said, like it was a major warning. She doubted there were any skeletons in his closet.

"Then you might as well tell me. That way, I'll hear your version," she said. She had no plans to discontinue this line of questioning until she got to the bottom of why she should know him. "Or would you rather the internet be the one to educate me?"

Chapter Seven

"First of all, don't believe anything you read about me on the internet." Tiernan was afraid of what Corinne Moore had printed about him in the society section of newspapers and blogs. Plus, he figured telling Melody something personal about himself might help her relax enough to get at least some sleep. She might not think she needed it or even be able to but he would do what he could to assist. "I used to be on the rodeo circuit."

"And now you have your own line of saddles?" she asked as her eyes widened. "Well, now I really am curious about your background. You must have been good at it considering sponsorships only go to the best."

"It's not a line, exactly," he said. "I have a workshop out back behind the house where I make custom saddles for individuals."

"As in one at a time?" she asked before her jaw fell slack.

"That's the deal," he said.

"They must cost a fortune," she said under her breath.

"Not exactly," he teased. "But close."

"Then, you must really be somebody for people to be willing to pay extra to have you make a saddle," she said with no hint of awe in her voice. She said the words as though she were reading the ingredients on a soup can.

That really made him laugh. He mainly dealt with rodeo folks who idolized him and treated him like something different than human. Like he didn't put his pants on one leg at a time like everybody else. Melody was a breath of fresh air.

"I did okay back in the day," he said.

"What does that mean? You aren't that old," she countered.

"I'm thirty-three," he said. "Pretty old in my world. Besides, I'm a little beat up. I decided to quit while I was still on top."

"Is that how you were able to hire John Prescott and have him show up on a moment's notice?" she asked. "Your fame?"

"Family connection helped there," he explained. "The Hayes name moves mountains in Texas despite Cider Creek being a small town."

"I'm not sure I've heard of Cider Creek," she admitted. "Is it far from Mesquite Spring?"

"It's about a thirty-minute ride from anywhere in the lower half of Texas," he said.

"That's impossible," she said in disbelief. The look on her face said she thought she was being played. "Texas is too big."

"Not by air," he said. "We have helicopters on standby near the ranch. Half an hour might be an exaggeration but it's not too far off base depending on who is holding the stick."

She gave a slight nod and he realized she must have grown up in a similar life of privilege. Tiernan may have butted heads with Duncan, but he realized how fortunate he'd been on the financial end.

"Your family has a lot of money," she hedged.

"Yes," he said. "Last I checked they did."

"Why not ride the gravy train?" she asked, and then a look of embarrassment heated her cheeks. "I'm sorry. That question was out of line. I just thought maybe you make two saddles a year and then live off your trust fund the rest of the time."

"I have no idea what's in my trust fund," he said.

"None?"

"I'm fully capable of earning a living on my own," he said with a little more ire than intended. He had to laugh at himself. As it turned out, the mention of living off a trust and not earning his own way still got him heated around the collar. Corinne, his ex, had been a Fort Worth socialite who never understood why he needed to work given his family name. She'd been charming and flirty in the beginning, until the socialite went for the jugular. "I set out to prove myself when I was eighteen years old and still wet behind the ears. I guess the subject is still a sore spot with me even though I've long since proven I can make my own way in life."

"You had a very successful rodeo career from the sounds of it," she said. The respect in her voice cut through some of his indignation. His pride had taken a hit at the suggestion he lived off a trust fund and couldn't make a life for himself.

"I'm doing all right by most standards," he said.

"Your cabin is beautiful," she said, glancing around. "Don't take this the wrong way but I'm a little surprised there aren't trophies everywhere."

"I saved a few that meant a lot to me," he said. "Those are in my workshop. I always thought it was important to separate who I am from what I do, if that makes any sense at all."

"Must have been tough sometimes," she continued. "Most people let all that fame go to their heads, it seems like."

"Ranchers aren't bred that way," he said.

"You wouldn't be able to tell a millionaire cattle rancher from one who struggles to make ends meet if you saw them walking down the street. Both would look you in the eye when they spoke and shake your hand."

"They must be some of the most grounded people on earth," she said. "Cider Creek sounds like a nice place to bring up a family."

"I haven't given it much thought," he admitted. "My siblings and I loved the land. Our mother is a saint for putting up with six kids."

"Six?" Melody barely got out the word. Her shock was written all over her face. "My mother had her hands full with two. Or maybe I should say it seemed difficult to juggle both us and all those glasses of wine."

He laughed at the image that popped into his thoughts. "I'm sure she did the best she could. The affair must have been hard on her."

"Not really," she said. "You think two people are in love because they're all you know until you realize your mother is more in love with a lifestyle. I think she was embarrassed more than anything else. An affair wasn't cause to leave. The first time my father had money issues was all it took for her to bolt. She used the affair as an excuse but that had happened two years earlier."

"Watching your family dissolve in front of

your eyes had to have been hard on you as a kid," he said.

She nodded before turning the tables. "What about your parents?"

"Father died when I was in middle school. Parents were high school sweethearts. They danced around the kitchen after supper." A knot of emotion formed in his throat at the memory. He'd blocked all those out years ago. "They were the real deal."

"I can't imagine how wonderful that must have been," she said wistfully. "I'm sorry for your loss."

"Thank you," he said. Her words brought a surprising amount of comfort. "It was hard on all of us. We didn't talk about him all that much anymore. Looking back, our mother must have been in terrible grief over losing the love of her life."

"I'm sad for her," Melody said as her hand covered her heart.

"I don't think she ever truly recovered despite being a strong person," he said. "There were cracks afterward, but we all knew she was doing her best. When it came to our relationship with our mother, we had a lot of love."

"That would be awful for anyone. The fact she survived and continued to bring up you and your siblings showed her true strength," she said.

Those words were balm to a wounded soul. He didn't realize how good it would feel to talk about his parents and what had happened in the past. Keeping everything locked inside for so long was like carrying a boulder on his chest. Remembering how much they'd loved each other lifted some of the ache.

But then it was easy to talk to Melody.

"Tell me more about your saddle business," Melody said, pushing up to sitting. Her long waves had dried and fell down her back and around her shoulders.

"Orders have kept me working fourteen-to eighteen-hour days leading up to Christmas, which will be here before we know it," he said, going with the change in topic.

"You've been off this entire day because of me," Melody said as she glanced at the clock on the mantel. "I should let you get back to work."

"Believe it or not, I've enjoyed getting to know you and doing something useful today," he said. "I've been at the saddles for the past couple of months straight with no break, and helping someone else brings me back to my roots. It's a rancher-like thing to do."

He could have sworn disappointment flashed in her eyes. He couldn't for the life of him fig-ure out why.

"Are there more people like you and your family in Cider Creek?" she asked, a wistful quality to her tone.

"All ranching communities have people like us," he said.

"Somehow I doubt that," she said so low that he had to strain to hear. Before he could respond, she said, "I should try to get some real sleep. Tomorrow is going to come early."

"Do you want me to work in another room?" he asked, not liking the wall that had just shot up between them. There wasn't a whole lot he could do about it, either.

"Whatever works for you," she said before adding, "But I'm good with things the way they are right now if it's too much trouble for you to leave."

Tiernan took the hint, picking up his laptop and rebooting. He made himself comfortable in the chair. A wall might have come up, but she trusted him enough to let him keep watch over her while she at least tried to sleep.

He pulled up orders and recalculated how much time he had left to finish them before Christmas. He'd intended to have everything delivered the day before Christmas Eve. Now, he'd lost a day, so he'd be working on Christmas Eve to get everything done on time.

On Christmas Day, he could collapse if he had to pull a few all-nighters. He could personally deliver at least one of the saddles, which would give him an extra day back since he didn't have to ship. He could finagle the order in which he completed the saddles and still make this work.

People were depending on him, and he never let them down. Could he make the same promise to Melody?

MELODY OPENED HER EYES, surprised she'd been able to fall asleep at all. The dim lighting in the room made it easy for her eyes to adjust. She glanced around the room to get her bearings. Her heart skipped a beat the second her eyes landed on Tiernan. The glow from his laptop cast shadows on his face that highlighted a strong jawline and cheekbones that could crack granite. The man was carved from perfection.

Her movement caused his gaze to shift to her. For a long moment, their eyes met, and it ranked right up there with one of the most intimate moments of her life.

"Hey," he said, his voice gravelly.

"Hi," she said, feeling like she could have thought of something better. As it was, her throat was suddenly dry, and forming words became a challenge. She cleared her throat. "What time is it?"

He glanced down at the corner of the screen and then his eyes came up again. She blinked to lessen the impact, but it was a fruitless attempt at best. She had the same reaction as a few seconds ago when their gazes touched.

This time, she took in a long, slow breath.

"Quarter after nine," he said.

"That late?" she asked, surprised. "How did I sleep so long?"

"You were out like a light, so I closed all the blinds. I figured you needed as much rest as possible," he said.

It occurred to her that she was wearing nothing but a bathrobe, so she performed a quick scan as she pulled the covers up. Relief flooded her when she confirmed nothing was out that shouldn't be. The only bare skin he might have seen was her foot and a sliver of ankle. In some cultures and periods in history, that was enough to be considered scandalous.

"Can I interest you in a cup of coffee?" Tiernan asked, setting the laptop down on the coffee table. Loki snored from the other side of the room until the piece of tech tapped the wood. The dog jumped to attention before launching himself toward the living area.

"Coffee would be nice," she said, still full from the lasagna last night. "Thank you."

"Not a problem," he said.

"Have you been on that thing all night?" She motioned toward the laptop.

"On and off," he admitted.

She sat cross-legged on the couch as Loki overshot and smacked into a wood coffee table. Thankfully, both dog and furniture were fine. The thud turned out to be the scariest part of the incident. His wagging tail was a whole tornado of its own.

Melody reached over and petted him. This dog understood the fire drill phrase, *stop, drop, and roll,* because that was exactly what he did. She recognized the maneuver from last night with the lawyer. "I know what this means." Loki wanted belly scratches. The bighearted pup really was growing on her. She wasn't ready to officially declare herself unafraid of large dogs, but Loki had wormed his way into her good graces a whole lot faster than she thought possible. His owner was making headway there, too, which was exactly the reason she needed to keep her guard up around him. On a soul level, she realized how deeply a man like Tiernan Hayes could hurt her.

He brought over a fresh cup. Their fingers grazed as he handed over the mug, causing more of those sensations to rocket through her.

Something had been niggling at the back of her mind since waking up. She took a few sips of coffee in an attempt to clear the coffers. She also realized she might be overstaying her welcome.

"Did you sleep last night?" she asked.

Tiernan shook his head.

"How are you still operating?" she asked. "I wouldn't be able to form sentences without at least a couple hours of sleep under my belt."

"You'd be surprised what growing up on a cattle ranch will do for you," he said on a chuckle. "During calving season, we got used to going two to three days without sleep. I don't even want to tell you all the places I was found asleep as a teenager."

Melody couldn't help but smile at the images of him, head back with his mouth open, passed out, rolling through her thoughts.

The niggling feeling returned. This time she knew what it meant.

"My brother made a point of saying he's been out of town for a few days trying to get his head straight about our father's case," she said.

"Was he setting up an alibi?" Tiernan asked.

"There's only one way to find out," she said. "But I don't think my lawyer would approve."

Chapter Eight

After hearing Melody's idea, Tiernan had no doubts Prescott wouldn't give the go-ahead.

"If I'm in the room with my brother, it'll be easier to tell if he's lying when I ask him where he was. His voice always shifts an octave when he's being untruthful and he doesn't blink as fast," she argued. Her point was valid. He just didn't think it was a good idea to put herself at risk.

"Reporters could be camped out in front of his home or office, or both," he pointed out. "At the very least, you'd be handing yourself over to the dogs, which doesn't seem like the right play."

"It's going to happen sooner or later," she argued.

"This thing could die down," he said. The sharp look she threw his way was the equivalent of a dart. He was grasping at straws to try to keep her from following through. "Then again, it might not. News in this area is few and far between. People could be chewing on this for a while."

"The case might be more cut-and-dried if a suspect was behind bars," she said. "As it is, people will think there's a killer on the loose and they will worry they might be next. That will keep interest in the story alive, and we all know where there's interest there will be almost constant coverage."

"No arguments from me there," he said. Corinne had set out to tarnish his reputation by spreading rumors he was a player and a boozer who would end up in the tabloids someday under the heading "Tiernan Hayes Falls from Grace." Melody's problem was on a much bigger scale. The stakes were higher. Attention would be on her for a long time to come.

"Plus, let's face it. I can't stay here much longer," she continued. "You have work to do. You must be behind after yesterday."

"I figured out a plan to catch up," he said as her gaze darted toward the exit.

"Which probably doesn't include having a houseguest," she said.

"It's no trouble on my end to have you here," he said, thinking she might have someone out there worried about her. She wasn't close with her family but that didn't mean she didn't have friends she could stay with or a guy. She hadn't looked at her phone once in the short time he'd known her, which didn't gel with what he knew of her workaholic life. It also led him to believe she was doing this on her own. "Unless someone else is out there concerned you haven't checked in."

She shook her head. "There's no one special. I work all the time as right hand to the owner of the company, so the few friends I used to have gave up on me a long time ago when I declined invite after invite."

"Working on your career is important," he said, able to relate a little too much to the scenario she described. He had buddies on the circuit. There were people he could call to go out for a beer who still believed in him. The thing about having any amount of fame was that women dated him for his name. A few he'd believed were actually interested in getting to know him turned out to be snapping incognito selfies.

Then he met Corinne. She'd done a number on him, and he'd shied away from dating ever since. Head down, a year passed before he realized he hadn't been on a date. All of which brought him to his current single status.

"I had a great interview yesterday," she said on a sharp sigh. "An offer was supposed to come through either last night or today."

"You haven't checked your phone to see," he said. "How do you know it didn't?"

"I'm afraid of my cell after what happened yesterday," she admitted. "The second news gets out that I'm somehow connected to a murder, my mother will freak out. My current boss most likely blew up my phone with texts, demanding to know where I am. The man has no boundaries. Well, not actually him but someone else in the office will get that assigned task. I know that I need to check in considering the fact I have responsibilities but I just can't right now."

"I don't blame you for not rushing toward that insanity," he said.

"It would be nice to know if I got the offer, though," she said. "I'm certain to lose my job and even if I don't, I can't go back there anymore. Not to work for a guy who thinks his college son can hit on me without any consequences."

Tiernan felt his jaw muscle clench. "That is the furthest thing from being acceptable."

"Tell my old boss that," she quipped. Then, she studied his face for a long moment. "On second thought, maybe not."

"I have a temper, but I'd never use it on someone," he defended. "I learned to keep it under control years ago when I saw the aftershocks. Sure, it might feel good in the moment to get out the rage with a willing participant. In the long run, it only ever made things worse. Broke relationships to the point they could never be repaired." He stopped himself right there before waxing too poetic.

She nodded. "I was angry with my father for so long and I just held it all inside. At some point, it becomes poison and you have to let it go."

"Have you?" he asked.

"I'm a work in progress on that one," she admitted. "Since my parents' divorce, it's been easy to restrict visits to holidays. I never have to stay long because I'm always off to the other person's house." She sat there, silent, for a moment that stretched on. "It occurs to me that I had a sibling I never met or knew about. How strange is that?"

"We might be able to get some information about the young man now that we have a name," Tiernan offered, picking up his laptop.

A host of emotions played out across her face before she settled on saying, "Let's do it and see what we come up with."

He moved to sit beside her so he could share the screen. Their outer thighs touched, causing heat to rocket through him. The urge to lean into it was darn near a physical ache the size of Texas sitting square on his chest. With her background, it was nothing short of a miracle she hadn't turned out to be a manipulative woman like Corinne. She'd had daddy issues worse than anything he'd seen, and he'd seen plenty. The impact a father had on his daughter had caused Tiernan to take note. Not that he planned on having kids anytime soon. They were a "one day" possibility that always seemed pushed into the future. At thirty-three and with no desire to get mixed up with another Corinne, he figured single life wasn't so bad. Being a bachelor had its perks. There was no one around to tell him not to watch a game on Sunday afternoon in the fall. Texas and football were right up there with God and country to most folks. He couldn't say he was as obsessed with the game as most in these parts, but he liked to watch the occasional battle on the gridiron.

He typed in Jason Riker and isolated the search to Texas. An Instagram account turned up at the top of the page. He clicked on the link. The first thing he noticed was the young man's face in the circle.

"He can't be out of high school yet, can he?" Melody asked. She must be thinking the same thing. "This makes everything so much worse."

Tiernan couldn't agree more.

"I recognize this woman," she said, pointing to one of the posts of what looked like mother and son. "And, look," she commented. "Her name is Bebe."

"Okay, let's see if we can figure out his age based on his posts," Tiernan said. There weren't many, which surprised him. He'd never gotten into the whole social media craze beyond hiring someone to manage a couple of pages for him, but young people seemed to be on it all the time.

He didn't have to scroll for long considering there were only eighteen posts.

"There's no hint of the kid except art he'd posted that looked like he'd done," she said out loud as she pointed to the picture. "What about tags?"

Tiernan hit the button, and then scrolled.

"You hit the nail on the head with your guess about his age," he said. "Look at this photo from June where this kid says she missed him at graduation in a comment."

"He's practically a baby," she said low and under her breath.

Tiernan nodded.

"Looks like he played soccer at one point," he said, scrolling down to a team photo with the words *best friends* as a caption.

"He left school before graduation? I wonder why?" Emotion came over her in a thick wave, threatening to drown her. She tucked her chin to her chest and sniffed, hiding the fact a few tears had spilled down her cheeks. The urge to thumb those droplets away was too great to ignore. So he reached over, electricity be damned, and did just that. He let his thumb linger on her chin as he tilted her head toward his. Her tongue darted across her bottom lip, leaving a silky trail, and it was as though a bomb detonated inside his chest. If he sat like this much longer, instincts were sure to take over. Before he could put a little space between them, Melody shifted her position enough to kiss him.

TIERNAN'S THICK LIPS tasted like dark roast, her new favorite flavor. His spicy scent flooded her senses, awakening something deep and primal within her. Need welled up and one word came to mind...*more*. She wanted more of Tiernan. More of his muscled arms around her, holding her. More of his rough, calloused hands roaming her body, reminding her she was alive. More of his weight on top of her, pressing her into a mattress, helping her get lost even for just a little while.

In this moment, she was in a haze and all she wanted was to lean into it, into him. So, she did. Melody parted her lips and teased his tongue inside her mouth. The low, throaty groan that tore from his lips only acted as more fuel. She lifted her hands to his shoulders and braced herself by digging her nails into his skin.

In the next second, Tiernan shifted their positions until he was on top of her, covering her with his heft. He balanced most of his weight on his arms and a knee that was acting as an anchor against the leather.

Her stomach felt like she was base jumping as he brought his chest flush with her body. Melody couldn't remember the last time she felt anything near this magnitude with a guy before. Was it the circumstances?

Did it matter? She was here. He was here. And all she wanted to feel was nothing but him, surrounding her, inside her, moving to their own tempo until the building tension found sweet release.

Tiernan abruptly stopped kissing her, but he didn't move. She gripped his forearms, willing him to stay right where he was for a little while longer.

"You're beautiful," he started, and she feared the rejection that was sure to come next. "But this can't happen."

Those four words were her least favorite from now on. She wriggled out from underneath him, making certain her robe didn't open in the process and reveal more of her than she intended. At least she was covered. "You're right." Her cheeks heated. If embarrassment could kill a person, she'd be dead. The minute she thought the words *kill* and *dead*, she wished she could take them back. Her heart ached for the kid. She forced her thoughts back to the current situation as she picked up her coffee cup and then took a sip.

What was this murderer doing here? Was he really coming for her? Or did he have questions? Questions about their father? About her? About Coop? The sheriff wasn't giving up information, so they needed to figure things out on their own.

When she looked over at Tiernan, she realized he was studying her. No matter how gorgeous this man was or how tempting those Cupid's bow lips were, she didn't have to touch a stove twice to remember it burned. She got the message loud and clear. *You're great, but...*

It didn't matter what came after the last word because everything she needed to know had been said right then and there. Practically throwing herself at a stranger, no matter how drop-dead beautiful, was crossing a line that she'd never once considered doing. Then again, she'd been running on instinct and pure need, and had gotten caught up in the moment. There would be no repeat.

"I won't ask if everything is okay," he said. "I won't waste your time with a stupid question."

He was dead on the nail there. Everything was most certainly not fine.

"I'm here instead of in my own home," she said. "This is a great place, but it's not mine. I have no idea what the sheriff and his deputies have done to my personal belongings. I probably should have been there to catalog what was taken, if anything." The idea someone could have planted her address in Jason's pocket struck like a physical blow. The same person might have put something in her home to tie her to the murder, which could also explain the note on her vehicle telling her to get away for a while. "Will Prescott check out the area where I was instructed to go?"

"I'm sure he already has someone on it. Probably already did after learning about it last night," he reassured.

She nodded.

"There are so many questions, and it feels like my life is on the line," she explained. The look on Tiernan's face was the same one from the sheriff's office yesterday. It was a mix of determination and frustration on her behalf. "I'd like to find out more about Jason, too. Where did he grow up? We have the name of the high school, but did he live in a house or apartment? Was his mother married or single? Did she work two jobs or live off a trust fund? How long did she know my father?" She calculated the math on the age difference between her and Jason. "I was fifteen years old when he would have been born. That's high school. The last name Riker doesn't ring any bells but the incident happened eighteen years ago."

"Do you think it would help to visit your father?" he asked.

"In jail?"

"Captive audience," Tiernan said.

She thought about it for a minute before responding. "You do make a point. It isn't like he can go anywhere." Even so, the idea of confronting her father about another affair was as appealing as sticking a butter knife through her eye sockets. "He could refuse to talk about it with me. Or, he could ask the guard to take him away."

"How long has it been since you've visited him?" Tiernan asked.

"I haven't," she said. "We have spoken on the phone. To be honest, I didn't think I could handle seeing my father locked behind bars. He hurt people, and I'll never forgive him for what he's done. People lost their homes and their savings because of him. But at the end of the day, he is still my father. That little girl tucked deep inside of me still wants this all to be a misunderstanding. And as long as I'm wishing, I might as well go all in and ask that my father turn out to be the hero six-year-old me believed in." In real life, people were flawed and sometimes jerks, and everything she believed she knew could be turned upside down in an instant with no rhyme or reason.

"Bad things happen to good people every day," he said after a thoughtful pause. "People can be damn disappointing."

"That sounds loaded," she said, flipping the tables. "Who let you down?"

Chapter Nine

Tiernan issued a sharp sigh. He opened his mouth to speak but then clamped it shut again. "Let's just say I've learned not to take people at face value. And when someone shows you their true colors, believe them. Don't stick around and give them second or third chances because you think you know them and convince yourself the signs aren't red flags."

It was the reason he'd stopped the kiss before he fell down that rabbit hole again. Besides, Melody had been through a traumatic experience and was most likely searching for proof of life. Nothing could happen between them. Not after he'd been burned.

"Sounds like there's a story behind those words," Melody said. Her eyebrow slightly arched.

"But with your parents, blind trust is usually the case," he continued, purposely not addressing her comment. He'd said too much already.

She studied him as she tilted her head to the right. He'd seen this look before. It seemed to be her go-to while she was deciding whether to push a subject or move on. After a slow sigh, she said, "I went all in with mine. Granted, I noticed that my mother was on the shallow side and my father could be superficial, but I kept making excuses for them in my mind. Like my dad just likes nice things and my mom enjoys friends and tennis more than carpool and baking cookies. I convinced myself that not every mother asked how their children's day was. Mine volunteered at school on a regular basis. She was on the PTA and kept close tabs on my grades."

"Those are acts of caring," he said.

"Looking back, I think mine and my brother's successes were her report card to our father," she countered. "It was as though she justified spending her days at the tennis club if she volunteered a couple of times a month at our school and we were the 'perfect' children. Once the money train stopped, she was out."

Tiernan knew women like that. In fact, he'd dated one. Corinne. All sparkle and no substance. "Mothers should be there for their children, offering unconditional love and support."

"Or be like me and just don't have kids," she said.

"Not everyone is cut out to be a parent," he

agreed. "But, somehow, I think you'd be different."

"How so?" she asked, her eyes widening in shock. "Why wouldn't I be exactly what my parents taught me to be? Cold and indifferent?"

"Because you're not built that way," he said. "For one, you could be living a whole lot more comfortable life but you chose to give it all away."

"In favor of earning it myself," she quickly added.

"Which speaks to your character," he pointed out.

She gave a reluctant-looking nod. "Speaking of family, I can't help but wonder if Jason's mother knew my father was married when they had an affair."

"No doubt, she is grieving the loss of her son, but I still think we should go talk to her and get the lay of the land," he said.

"Agreed. Do you think we could stop off at my house first?" she asked. "I'd like to get clothes and check out the damage after the law searched my apartment."

"We can do that," he said. "Is there a back door, by chance?"

"No. I live in an apartment on top of a UT professor and his wife's garage," she said.

"Then, we'll have to play it straight," he said.

Her expression twisted, so he added, "I'll do everything I can to protect you from reporters or bloggers. If we're lucky, they'll assume you're not coming back and take off."

"Sounds almost too good to hope for," she said.

"It probably is but we'll charge ahead anyway." A hoodie would help so she could hide as much of her long russet locks as possible. They could be tucked inside. Sunglasses would shield at least some of her face. "I have a hoodie you can wear that should swallow you whole."

"That should help hide me," she said. "What about bottoms? All I have is the skirt I wore yesterday."

"My ex was about your size," he said. "She left a few pieces of clothing that I didn't have time to donate, even though they've been sitting here six months." He stopped short of retracting the offer when he realized how much he didn't like the visual of her in Corinne's clothing. "Your undergarments are in the dryer. At least those are yours." He also didn't need the image of her silky pink panties stamped in his thoughts, especially when his mind wandered to envisioning her wearing them. The matching silk bra didn't help matters, either.

"That would be nice," she said. "I don't want

to wear my interview outfit, and the baggy clothes should help me hide."

He nodded. "I'll get your things." He stood up. "Are you hungry?"

"I could probably eat," she said. "I *should* try to get something down before we head out." She stood up and then paused. "You know, rather than speak to my father first, I'd like to find Bebe Riker and hear her side of the story. My father is a master manipulator and liar, and I'd like to go in with as many of my ducks in a row as possible."

"Sure," he said. "I'll dig around on the kid's Instagram and see what I can find out about her."

"Do you think Prescott already did? Shouldn't we just ask him?"

"I'd like to stay under the radar with our actions until we find something worth sharing," he said. "Prescott will definitely do his own investigation with a small army to help. Having you follow the trail might spark something. It's possible you've seen Bebe before hanging around and it just hasn't clicked yet. The same could be said for Jason. This could be the first time he was coming to you. Maybe being around his mother or seeing some of his things will stir something. You never know."

"Will you be okay to slack off work today?" she asked. "We have a lot of plans, and it sounds like it's going to take a good chunk out of your day to follow through on all this. I don't want to take you away from your livelihood."

"I'll figure it out," he reassured. There was no way he was letting her do this alone if she was willing to accept his help. One person was dead and they had no way to narrow down possible suspects. At this point, everyone they came into contact with had to be treated like a threat.

"If you're sure," she said, doing that thing with her head while she studied him.

"Scout's honor," he promised.

"Why don't I believe you were ever a Boy Scout?" she asked.

His response came in the form of a chuckle. He clamped his mouth shut and then walked into his bedroom to grab the clothes. He needed to finish getting dressed, too. After he threw on a shirt and socks, and then located Corinne's sweatpants, he headed into the living room. "Give me five minutes to feed Loki and let him out before we grab a bite and then take off."

"It'll take me that long to get myself together," she said with a small smile before taking the offerings and heading toward the guest room.

Loki was winding up to his usual overactive self. Tiernan fed his dog while he thought about whether or not it was a good idea to bring Loki along for the day. Leaving him here alone was a recipe for disaster. Tiernan could grab a leash and water container so he could tie Loki to a tree while they visited the prison. That trip might not happen today, though, depending on how it went with the other two stops. She was right about one thing. They had an entire day planned with all the driving involved. It occurred to him they would have to check prison visitation hours since it wouldn't be a drop-in situation.

After filling his dog's bowl, he walked over to the sliding glass door and opened it. Loki was a well-oiled machine at this point when it came to bolting outside and doing his business despite the occasional squirrel chase. After what happened yesterday, Tiernan stood at the door and kept watch.

The hairs on the back of his neck pricked as he looked out onto his yard. He surveyed the land. Was someone out there? Watching?

MELODY TOOK A step into the living area and then froze. The look on Tiernan's face as he looked out onto the backyard caused her stomach lining to braid and a knot to form in her chest. She cleared her throat so she wouldn't startle him. "Everything okay?"

The first clue he was concerned was the way he stood at the door with his hands fisted at his sides, tensed up like he was ready for a fight.

"I'm just watching Loki," he said without a glance in her direction. It was her second clue he was on guard.

"Mind if I join you?" she asked, figuring his answer would be a good gauge at how worried she should be.

"No," he said. The third clue was how quickly his answer came. His arm extended out like when a driver stepped on the brakes too hard, and their arm flew out to shield their passenger from being thrown into the dashboard. Then, he called Loki's name with the same authoritative voice as someone in law enforcement who'd walked into a hot situation.

The knot in her chest tightened as she stood rooted to her spot. She glanced around, looking for anything she could use as a weapon. Her gaze landed on a fireplace poker. If anything went down, she wanted to be prepared.

A few seconds later, the black Lab came bolting through the glass doors, but Tiernan didn't immediately shut them. Instead, he took a step to block the opening with his heft. He stood there, arms crossed over his chest and his feet apart in an athletic stance.

Rather than work herself up to full freak-out, she decided to check out the fridge to see if there was anything easy to grab. Food might prove a good distraction and there were knives in the kitchen she could use if needed.

At the moment, she was a ball of anxiety just thinking about law enforcement officers picking through her personal belongings, going through her home. The helpless feeling took her back to standing in the doorway to her English teacher's room when her father had his slacks around his ankles and her teacher bent over a desk. The grunts still echoed in her head and made her sick to this day. She'd spent years trying to block the image that had a way of popping into her thoughts every time she saw her father.

Melody tried to shake off the gross feeling. That day, the perfect family of four image had exploded like a watermelon being tossed onto a summer sidewalk. Except there'd been no way to clean up the shattered pieces.

She sighed, doing her best to force the memory out of her mind as she focused on the contents of the fridge as she opened the door. The inside was surprisingly organized for a bachelor. She'd clearly been dating the wrong guys because she was lucky to find a box of cold pizza and beer in theirs.

For a split second, her mind went to Tiernan having a woman in the background. Then, she remembered he did. A house cleaner.

Containers were neatly stacked and filled with

food that looked delicious. There was a container of milk and another filled with orange juice. She searched for eggs, grated cheese and maybe some chives. After locating the items, she loaded her arms.

Turning around, she nearly plowed into Tiernan. The solid wall of a man caught her by the arms, and then held her steady until she regained composure.

"Are you okay?" he asked, dipping his head down until he found her eyes. Locking on was a big mistake on her part if she was going to keep from kissing the man again.

"Fine," she muttered, hearing the shakiness in her own voice. "Is it all good outside?" She could play off her nerves as being concerned there was an intruder on his property. Would he buy it?

"False alarm," he said, letting go of her arms. The absence of him was immediate when he took a step backward. "But I'd rather be safe than sorry."

"I couldn't agree more," she said, turning toward the counter near the stove. "Mind if I whip up some eggs?"

"Sounds good to me," he said. The only hint that he was as affected as she'd been came when his voice cracked. He coughed to cover. "I can help or do a little digging to find out more about Bebe."

"We'll get things done faster if we divide and conquer," she said. Putting distance between them seemed like a good idea right now. The temperature in the kitchen had gone from moderate to blazing hot a minute ago.

He nodded, hesitated like he was about to say something, and then shook his head as he walked off.

Melody got busy rinsing and chopping green onions. His kitchen was orderly and intuitive. What it lacked in size, it made up for in ease. Everything she needed was within reach. She remembered milk, so she grabbed the container from the fridge. After whisking all the ingredients, aside from the cheese, she turned the heat on the gas range and located a suitable pan. A loaf of bread sat next to the fridge and she'd spotted a toaster. While the eggs worked in the pan, she made toast. Finding jelly in the fridge was the equivalent of hitting the lotto.

Plates were filled in a matter of minutes. She brought them over to the granite island and set them down near the stools. She skipped one so she wouldn't have to sit so close to Tiernan that she could smell his spicy male scent. Getting too used to it, to him, would be a fatal mistake to her heart.

Loki made a bed right next to her feet as she claimed her spot. Tiernan walked over, laptop in hand. He glanced at her and then his plate but didn't comment on the distance in between. The dog was growing on her, too.

"I found information on Bebe," Tiernan said, keeping his gaze on the screen. He positioned it so she could see. "She's the morning manager at Green Things Grocery in Lake Thickett."

"Where is that?" she asked.

"It's in between Cider Creek and Austin," he supplied.

She shot him a confused look. "You've talked about Cider Creek, but I'm still not sure where it is."

"It's northeast of Austin," he said. "GPS will give us the exact distance but it's safe to guess an hour to an hour and a half."

"And the grocery?" she continued. "I'm guessing that's in town."

He nodded before pulling up the grocer's website. "They open at 6:00 a.m. and close by eight thirty."

"I can scarcely imagine living somewhere they roll up the streets by nightfall," she said with an involuntary shift that made Tiernan chuckle.

"Not everyone is cut out for the country," he said.

"I wouldn't exactly call Austin cosmopolitan," she countered.

"True," he said as he picked up his plate. A wall had come up after the kiss even though chemistry still pinged between them. He didn't seem like the type to let himself go there again once a door closed.

It was a shame they hadn't met under different circumstances. Tiernan Hayes was the kind of person she could see herself with—*really* see herself with. It was next to impossible to erase the kiss that had been burned into her mind and body. Just thinking about it caused her lips to sizzle.

Since focusing on the sexual chemistry—sex she was certain would blow her mind—was as productive as trying to run through fire and not come out burned, she shifted. The dishes were done in a matter of minutes as Tiernan gathered supplies for Loki.

Green Things Grocery was their second stop. Surprising a grieving mother wasn't high on Melody's list of good ideas. One part of her wanted answers about the current case. Then again, a grieving mother might take off work the day after learning her son was murdered. Another part of her wanted to see what another one of her father's conquests looked like in person. The question of why their family hadn't been enough to make the man happy had haunted her since high school. Why did young people always blame themselves for everything that happened? Because she'd convinced herself that if she'd been a better student or had made him proud he would have cared more about them.

The revelation caught her off guard. She hadn't allowed herself to think in those terms, since she'd been too young to know better. Hearing it as an adult made her realize how silly it had been to hold on to that hurt for this long. It wasn't her job to make her parents happy or keep them married. She could see that so clearly now. Strangely, a weight she'd been carrying around for the better part of her adulthood was slowly lifting.

"Ready to head to your place and get the lay of the land?" Tiernan asked, pausing at the door with Loki at his side.

"As much as I'll ever be," she conceded, unsure how it would feel to walk into her apartment or come face-to-face with her father's mistress. She was about to find out the answer about both.

Melody followed Tiernan outside and into his dual cab pickup.

The drive to her place took an hour. Tiernan circled the block. Austin had foot traffic at pretty much all hours of the day and night thanks to the University of Texas at Austin. Fifty thousand students meandering through downtown kept the area lively.

Tiernan exited the pickup after leashing Loki. The pair came around to her side and then opened the door for her. She still hadn't checked her cell phone, trying to avoid pain as long as possible.

As soon as she exited the pickup, Tiernan reached for her hand. Slipping her hand into his palm brought on a surprising wave of calm. She didn't want to think about how incredible those calloused hands would feel roaming over her exposed skin.

Between holding hands and having a dog on a leash, they were probably a convincing-looking couple to outsiders. She brought her free hand up to grip his arm while she leaned into him. In a surprising move, he dipped his head and kissed her.

"That should sell it," he said in a whisper, but his raspy voice gave away the affect the kiss had on him. The moment his lips had closed down on hers, her heart engaged in a freefall. It would be so easy to get lost in Tiernan.

They climbed the stairs outside the garage, hand in hand. The wooden stairs groaned underneath Tiernan's weight. Loki trailed behind, trying to wind through their legs. She could only imagine what her landlord must think of her right now. Thankfully, she didn't see his car in the garage. He should be at work by now. His wife traveled during the week, so Melody wasn't worried about her showing up.

She pulled out her key ring, which had too many bobbles on it. They made it easier to find in her purse but also heavier. Plus, she'd collected them from various life events, making it difficult to throw them away. Each bobble was a reminder of a place she'd visited. Out of the corner of her eye, in the crack of wood under her foot, she saw metal glint against the sun.

Melody bent down and picked it out from between the slats. "What is this?"

Tiernan took a knee. "What the hell?"

The bloody locket was opened just enough for her to see her and Coop's pictures inside.

Chapter Ten

Tiernan didn't like the looks of this. He glanced around to see if anyone was particularly interested in the two of them. The locket was evidence they needed to turn over to Prescott. "Be careful in case a fingerprint can be lifted."

He ushered a silent Melody into the apartment after she fumbled with the keys to unlock the door. After a quick check around the living room to make sure the home was secure, he closed and locked the door behind them.

Loki must have picked up on Tiernan's mood because his ears went up on full alert. He froze except for his tail, which always had a mind of its own, wagging like crazy. Nerves kicked the swishing movement into high gear. Right now, he was in overdrive.

Melody tossed the piece of jewelry on the counter and took a step back. She'd long since dropped his hand. He missed the feel of her delicate skin against him. She would probably laugh at the description because she was one of the strongest people he knew. But her skin was like touching silk.

"I need to let Prescott know about this," he said, pulling out his phone. He snapped a picture of the "present" before shooting over a text to the lawyer. "Let's leave that alone until we get instructions on how to move forward."

"Okay," she said with a hollow quality to her voice that brought out his protective instincts. "I'll just grab an overnight bag and throw some clothes inside."

He nodded as she excused herself.

"Hold on," he said before she entered the hallway. He held out Loki's leash. "Take him with you."

A flash of relief passed behind her eyes as she took the offering. Tiernan planned to join them in a minute after he scoped out the place and made sure the area was secure. Law enforcement didn't exactly turn her apartment upside down. There were a couple of bills scattered on top of the counter. The place looked picked through but not ravaged. Throw pillows had been tossed onto the couch rather than neatly placed. A few drawers were ajar.

Tiernan walked through the living area and into the small but efficient kitchen. Her apartment had a clean but feminine look. Her furniture was in mostly neutral tones with soft throw pillows. The round marble table against one wall in the kitchen had two chairs that looked like something he'd find in one of those cool cafés. Modern? Contemporary?

Either way, he could see himself comfortable here. There were a few plants to give the place enough green. Other than that, the look was simple.

Once he'd checked in the pantry and behind doors, he moved into the hallway. There were essentially three doors. The first one on the right housed a washer and dryer. The second was a bathroom with all the essentials. The third was a reasonably sized bedroom. The decorating carried over from the living room and kitchen. The platform bed had a cloth headboard. There was an overnight bag sprawled out on top of the covers.

Loki came running toward Tiernan as he entered the room. His run was abruptly halted when the slack ran out of the leash. Rather than get her arm jerked out of its socket, Melody let go.

"Hey, buddy. Sit," Tiernan said, but this wasn't one of those times Loki could calm down enough to obey. Tiernan balled his fist and raised it to chest level. The hand signal had a better success rate once Loki hit a certain level of energy.

It worked. He plopped his butt on the wood flooring.

"Good boy," Tiernan reassured.

All the drawers in this room were closed at this point. Only the closet door was still open. He imagined Melody had gone through and straightened up the place.

"Have you noticed anything missing so far?" he asked.

She shook her head. "I keep important papers inside the nightstand. They all look to be in order."

"The law would be looking for a weapon or possibly your laptop," he said.

"Oh. Right," she said. "I guess I should have been looking around for that. The necklace freaked me out, and just seeing anything out of place like drawers still being opened when I walked in is strange. Knowing people were in here without my permission." She shuddered. It was easy to see the physical impact in her body language. The mental had to be twice as rough.

Loki heard a noise. He whirled around toward the window, giving the sound his full attention.

"It might be nothing, but we should get out of here as soon as possible," Tiernan said as he followed the dog over to the window. He kept out of view in case someone was downstairs watching, leaning his back against the wall beside the curtain.

After a few seconds ticked by with all three of them frozen, save for Loki's swishing tail, Tiernan risked a glance. Whatever the dog heard must be gone now. For all he knew, it could have been a bird or squirrel in a nearby tree. Dogs had far more sensitive ears than humans.

"Looks okay out there," he said to Melody.

She immediately jumped into action, filling the last of the space in the overnight bag. After zipping it up, she shouldered the strap. Tiernan met her in the middle of the room and took the bag from her.

"I'll just take a quick look around," she said. "To be fair, I usually keep my laptop on my bed because I check email at night. The fact that it's not here means the sheriff's office must have confiscated it." She issued a sharp sigh. "Is that even allowed?"

"If they have a search warrant signed off on by a judge, I'm afraid they can take anything they view as evidence," he said, thinking he needed to update Prescott. Although, the lawyer most likely already assumed the worst. Lawyers were good at that in Tiernan's experience. The good ones decided everything that could go wrong on the case already had.

He followed Melody into the next room where

she scanned the place. She walked over to the scattered mail, swept it up with her hand and then dropped it inside her purse.

"I don't know how I'm supposed to pay my bills without my laptop," she said on a frustrated sigh. "My accounts aren't on my phone."

"We'll sort it out back at my place if you'd like to stay over again," he promised, fully expecting her to reject the offer.

"Okay," she said with a look of relief. "Then, I won't panic about my electricity being turned off because I didn't pay the bill on time. My brain is scattered right now and I suddenly can't remember if it's due or if I paid it."

"I have to get some work done in my shop this evening," he started. "I can always lend you a laptop. You can come out there with me if you don't want to be in the house alone."

Her gaze widened and she tilted her head. "You wouldn't mind?"

"No trouble at all," he said. The relief in her eyes was all the thanks he needed. Besides, he actually liked being around her. This way, he could kill a few birds with one stone.

"At first blush, it looks like the laptop is the only major item the sheriff's office took," Melody said after giving the living room and kitchen a once-over. "If something was planted here before they showed up, that's a whole different conversation."

There was a lot about her situation that seemed orchestrated. For instance, the note on her vehicle being left the same day the body was found. Could it be a coincidence? Was someone in the know? Her brother came to mind. They were going to have to speak to Coop.

Prescott hadn't returned Tiernan's text with instructions on how to handle the locket, and Tiernan sure as hell wasn't leaving it behind. He'd watched a crime show with Corinne once where a detective placed evidence in a paper bag.

"Do you use paper or plastic?" he asked her as she stood at the door with her hand on the handle, a clear sign she was more than ready to get out of there.

"At the grocery?" she asked. "Paper."

"Where do you save the empties?" he asked.

She motioned toward the sink. "In the cabinet under there."

Tiernan retrieved a folded-up bag from the stack. Using a paper towel, he picked up the necklace and placed it inside. "We'll have to run this by Prescott's office while we're downtown before we head over to Green Things."

"Okay," she said. Her quick, overly enthusiastic response said she dreaded facing down her father's one-time mistress. She couldn't avoid it for very long. The stop with the necklace would only add an extra twenty minutes in between here and the grocer, where he hoped to get a few answers.

MELODY SAT IN the pickup with Loki while Tiernan ran into the law office. She could see the receptionist through a wall of windows from their parking spot in front of the downtown Austin building, making it easy to keep an eye on Tiernan. There was something comforting about having him in her line of sight at all times after being in her apartment. The awful feeling of her home being violated returned, washing over her like a rogue wave threatening to suck her under and drown her.

Then there was her half-brother, Jason. Facing his mother while she was reeling from the loss of her child made Melody sick to her stomach. There was no getting around the visit. It had to happen, so she would put on her "big girl" pants and push through.

Another minute passed before Tiernan was back in the driver's seat. At least they'd handed off the locket. An involuntary shiver rocked her body. Where had it come from? Who did it belong to?

"I should have taken a picture of the locket before you turned it in," Melody said to Tiernan.

"It's on my phone," he said with a raised eyebrow as he checked to see if a car was behind them.

"Right," she said. "I forgot."

He backed out of the spot and navigated into traffic. She should probably check her own phone at this point. She had time to kill between now and arriving at the grocer. This might be a good opportunity to get through some of her messages and voice mails. Most of them would be work related. Since she was most definitely fired after not showing up yesterday and today, she might as well face the music and get it over with.

After retrieving and turning on her cell, she took a good look at the screen. The button indicating texts showed the number fifty-seven. Her email icon showed double the number. The second wasn't a huge surprise, considering she was the communication gatekeeper for a real-estate tycoon. She would take great pleasure in being able to hand off all those to someone else. There was always a backup in case she needed to take a morning off to attend something like jury duty. Pamela Steiner was that person.

Rather than go through each email, Melody clicked the button beside every name she recognized and forwarded the lot directly to Pamela. She typed a quick note welcoming Pamela to the position. She'd made no secret of wanting the job when Melody moved on at some point. HR had been on a cross-training kick for the past two years. Looked like their efforts were about to pay off big-time.

There were half a dozen emails left from folks she didn't know. One by one, she clicked through them. Four were work related. One was spam that had gotten past her filter and managed to land in her inbox. The other contained a pointed message.

"Hey, I got something creepy in my spam folder," she said to Tiernan as she studied her cell.

"What is it?" he asked.

"'You did this and now you'll pay,'" she said as she read the screen. Ice water ran cold down her back.

"That's direct," he said. "Forward it to Prescott. He'll need to see it."

"The words aren't the worst part," she said. "It came from my mother's inbox but there's no way she sent it. For starters, it would be the first time she emailed me. I highly doubt she would start now."

"Someone could have easily phished her email," he said. "It doesn't require the most top-notch hacking skills if they can get someone to click on a link. Then, they can send a note from their 'inbox' remotely."

"My mom knows how to use her iPhone six ways past Tuesday, but I could see her falling for a scammer when it came to emails," she said. "All it would take is something happening with my brother for her to immediately click."

"Hackers have gotten good at tricking folks," he said. "I fell for it one time and got locked out of my email. That was a long time ago. I learned my lesson."

"It only takes once," she agreed. "Do you have Prescott's email handy, by the way?"

"It's in my phone," he said, fishing it out of his pocket before handing it over. "You're welcome to check my contacts."

Tiernan's gaze locked on to something or someone in the rearview as he handed over the cell.

"I need your thumb," she said, noticing the tension lines on his face as he bounced back and forth between the road in front of him and whatever he was keeping an eye on behind them.

"Just enter the code, instead—111111," he said.

She entered the numbers and then glanced over at him. "Everything okay?"

"We have a tail," he said. "What I'm trying

to determine is whether it's law enforcement or someone to be worried about."

Those words weren't exactly reassuring. Going home might have been a mistake. They'd found the locket, though. It made her wonder if the person who'd dropped it had arrived after the law. Wouldn't an investigator find the piece of silver jewelry? Granted, it had been wedged in between wood slats, and the sun was just right to cause a glint that had caught her eye. The law might have been focused on getting inside her place rather than scanning the outside. And yet, wouldn't they be more thorough?

She'd read news stories of high-profile investigations where officers and deputies had mishandled evidence. There'd been other cases where key pieces of evidence had been introduced late in the game from the original crime scene or couldn't be used because it had been trampled on by an officer. It happened.

Another explanation was the sheriff had made up his mind she was guilty and went in mostly looking for her laptop to confiscate. He might have instructed his deputies to take certain items. Someone had gone through her mail. She never left it scattered around on the countertop.

It was probably good that she wasn't home when they'd searched the place. Of course, her landlord probably let them in. She would have some explaining to do once this was all over.

She located Prescott's contact information and then forwarded the email to him. There was a small sense of accomplishment that came with clearing her inbox despite the scary message. It dawned on her to check the date the message came in.

"Three days ago," she said out loud.

"The sheriff will check your phone logs and your emails, so I don't feel a sense of responsibility to pass the message along," Tiernan said.

"Good point," she said. "Is there anything they won't touch?"

"You, as long as I'm breathing," he said so low she almost didn't hear it. The reassurance helped calm her nerves a notch below panic. Was it a promise he could keep?

Melody checked the time. The ride over to Green Things took an hour and twenty minutes. Before Melody realized it, the truck was parked in the lot and she stared at a green and white building.

"I'll crack the windows and leave Loki inside since it's chilly," Tiernan said. "Are you ready to go inside and meet Bebe Riker?"

"No," Melody said. "But I don't see how there's any other choice."

Chapter Eleven

Bebe Riker stood in the middle of the store in front of a grand Christmas display. The holiday was a couple of weeks away and she was already supervising the deconstruction of the elaborate presentation, shifting to what looked like an endcap display instead. Long black hair pulled off her face in a ponytail, she was the shell of a woman who was most likely a former beauty queen.

Melody froze the minute her eyes landed on Bebe. She reached for Tiernan's hand, most likely for reassurance. He didn't care what the reason was because linking their fingers felt good to him, like when a puzzle piece that had been lost was found and fit perfectly.

For a second, he wondered if Melody would chicken out and head right back out the door. Instead, she just stood there. Staring. There had to be half a dozen emotions playing through her mind. Facing her father's mistress—a mistress who'd had his child—had to be one of the worst things she'd ever do.

Bebe turned around and caught them watching her. She did a double take, giving away the fact she recognized Melody. A long pause where no one moved passed before Bebe issued a sharp sigh, barked orders at the pair of high-school-age boys breaking apart the exhibit and then stormed toward them.

Melody's grip tightened before she let go of Tiernan's hand altogether. She tensed, ready for the squall headed their way. Bebe stopped a couple of feet in front of them.

"My name's Tiernan," he said, trying to deflect some of the tension. He held out his hand. Bebe took it and gave a polite handshake.

"I'm Melody," she said. "But I think you already know that."

Bebe nodded, not offering her name in return. "What brings you to my part of town?" The way she said those words, then crossed her arms over her chest gave Tiernan the impression Bebe decided she was from the wrong side of the tracks when it came to the Cantors. Then again, Melody's dad might have pointed out the fact on his way out the door. The bastard.

"Your son," Melody said.

Bebe started tapping her toe against the sterile white flooring. Red-rimmed brown eyes sized them up. "Well, he's gone, so you're wasting your time." The older woman's chin quivered but no tears formed in her eyes. The toe tapped faster. "I'm only here today because I didn't know what else to do with myself."

Despite putting up a tough front, everything else about her body language said she was broken. Was Jason's death the reason? Or was his murder the straw that broke the camel's back?

"I'm sorry," Melody said with the kind of compassion that would normally melt a glacier in the dead of winter.

Tap. Tap. Tap.

The toe tapping sped up.

"He didn't deserve what happened to him," Melody continued. "I don't have children, so I won't pretend to know what you're going through."

"Then don't."

"I was hoping to talk to you, but I understand if you can't—"

"It was only a matter of time with the track he was on," Bebe said through clenched teeth. Even though her beauty had faded, remnants remained. Her hair still had a shine that made it look raven-like. Her face was heart shaped and her eyes big and brown. There was a dullness to them now but he could see where they would have been beautiful when they sparked. She was slim, but hints of curves remained. Although she was mad right now, it was easy to see that she wasn't hardened. It was more like tired. Heavy. Like she carried the weight of the world on her shoulders. There was no wedding ring or tan line where a band would have been, giving the impression she'd been a single mother. A tough road. His own mother had brought up six children on her own while living on her father-in-law's ranch. At least she had her mother to pitch in. Still, Tiernan and his siblings would qualify as a handful.

"I'm sorry I didn't know about him until now," Melody said.

"I'm not surprised," Bebe bit out. She ground her back teeth as the clank of a metal reindeer smacked against the tile behind her. "I have work to do and we're not exactly family, so…"

"Jason deserved better from my father," Melody said. "He was a bastard for treating people the way he did."

"Heard he was in jail," Bebe said with unbridled animosity in her tone. She turned before Melody could respond. "Serves him right."

Melody caught Bebe by the arm. "It does." Bebe froze and slanted a death stare on Melody's hand. "But Jason didn't deserve what happened to him. I'd like to talk to you about it because all the women around my father are treated like throwaways, including me."

Bebe didn't meet Melody's gaze. She stood still for what seemed like minutes.

"I'm the wrong person to ask for help," she said with finality as she jerked away from Melody's grip.

Melody glanced over at Tiernan, and then they retraced their steps to the pickup where Loki sat. Tiernan opened the door, and the rambunctious pup jumped out. He ran over to a patch of grass and did his business before hauling back.

"Good boy," Tiernan said as Melody reclaimed the passenger seat.

"That was useless," Melody said. "All I did was cause that woman more pain. My family has done enough to her. I shouldn't have come here."

"Mind if I let Loki run in the field next door for a few minutes?" Tiernan asked, figuring the dog had sat inside the cab and been good long enough. His energy was ramping up and needed release before they made the trek home.

"Of course not," she said. "He's been so good. Besides, it'll give me a chance to get through some of these texts."

Tiernan called Loki after grabbing a tennis ball from the back seat. Loki came roaring over. Thankfully, the lot was empty save for two cars parked up closer to the front door. He'd intentionally parked far away in case Loki bolted when the doors opened.

As Tiernan cut across the parking lot toward the field, he saw Bebe standing at the window, hands on her hips, looking in the direction of the truck.

MELODY'S NERVES WERE on edge. Tiernan's presence had kept her calm enough to follow through with talking to Bebe, but staring into those dull brown eyes had pierced her. Knowing her father had broken more than just her family caused a knot to form, braiding her stomach lining. Even though she realized none of it was her fault, she couldn't help feeling like dirt for his actions. The man had hurt so many people. Guilt slammed into her at ever believing in him, thinking he might be a decent human being after all.

On a sigh, she glanced down at her cell phone and the number of texts she was facing with no desire to read any of them. The promise of feeling better after clearing the deck was the only reason she pushed forward.

A knock on the window startled her. A gasp escaped before she could suppress it. A woman stood next to her. Bebe.

The window was cracked but the pickup was turned off. Melody motioned for Bebe to take a step back. She complied.

"Hey," Melody said as she exited on the passenger side.

Bebe clamped her mouth shut, and for a second, Melody wondered if the grocery manager would decide coming out here had been a bad idea and bolt back into the store. Her eyes said she had something to say.

"You really didn't know about us?" Bebe asked.

"No," Melody said a little defensively. She glanced over at Tiernan in the field who was watching with interest. Having him there was nice even though it was a temporary arrangement. "I distanced myself from my father when I caught him in the act cheating on my mother with my high school English teacher."

"Ouch," Bebe said, twisting her face in discomfort as if she'd been the one to walk in on them.

"You could say it scarred me," Melody admitted, letting a little bit of her guard down with Bebe.

"I'd say," Bebe added. She twisted her fingers together. "Jason always wanted a sister."

"I wish I'd known him," Melody said as a rogue tear escaped. She apologized.

"Don't ever say you're sorry for having an emotion," Bebe said. "I wish I could cry. It might make me feel better to get some release." She shook her head. "All I get is dry eyes and a heart that feels like a thundercloud that can't rain."

Acting on pure instinct, Melody leaned in and hugged Bebe. Her body stiffened at first, but then she relaxed into it.

"Thank you for that," Bebe said when Melody let go. "I still haven't given the coroner instructions on where to send the…*him*, after they release him. I just can't believe he's gone. When I look at the front door, I expect him to come bursting through. His hair was always in need of a cut. He was a mess this year after he decided to locate the bastard who walked away from us."

"Why now? Why after all this time?" she asked, hoping the reason could give a hint as to who his real killer was. Could her father have been afraid his secret was about to get out?

"It was about six months ago," Bebe said. "Jason said he didn't want to graduate high school without knowing who his father was." She braided her fingers again. "I warned him that he would be disappointed." She flashed eyes at Melody. "Henry told me straight out that he wanted nothing to do with the kid after I told him I was pregnant."

There were so many words that came to mind at this moment. She wanted to unleash them on her father.

"Before that, he made me feel like the most

beautiful person in the world," Bebe said, a wistful quality to her tone. "I was younger then. Naive, I guess. I fell hook, line and sinker. When he told me that I couldn't come to his house for dates because he was caring for an ailing mother, I didn't see that as a red flag. I think it made him look noble in my eyes."

"How old were you when the two of you got involved?" Melody asked.

"Nineteen," Bebe said. Barely older than Melody at the time. This made her sick. She'd once broken off a friendship with a girl named Leslie who said she didn't like sleeping over at Melody's house because of the way her father looked at her. Melody had jumped to his defense. Now, she wanted to give Leslie a call and apologize. How could her father be such a jerk, and Melody not see it sooner?

"That's so young," Melody said.

Bebe nodded. "He was older than me. Obviously. I believed his story that his wife and kids were killed in a boating accident on Lake Travis. It made me fall even harder for him, but then I used to bring home every stray animal, too. Turns out, I'm a sucker for a sob story."

"Good people believe others," she said. "It's a sign you were a nice person."

"I hope something good can come out of this," Bebe said. "It's been nothing but heartache since the day I found out I was pregnant." She glanced up. "Oh, don't get me wrong. I loved my kid with all my heart. And your dad, too. I never would have slept with someone without falling for them."

"You were manipulated, pure and simple," Melody pointed out. "He preyed on you because you were young, and he could. He can be convincing, too. Believe me, I know better than most. The man had me believing we were the perfect family for most of my life."

"You were a child," Bebe said. "There were so many red flags. I should have known better."

"Signs only work when we know to look for them," Melody countered.

Bebe nodded and some of the weight in her eyes lifted. "That's a real fair point." She worked her fingers. "I guess I owe you an apology for the way I treated you when you first showed up."

"Not necessary," Melody said. "But I would like to know more about Jason. We looked at his social media page. He seemed like he was thriving before he went to find my dad."

"He was a good kid." Bebe sighed and gave an exasperated look. The kind of frustration that came from a mother who couldn't quite figure out what had happened to her child. It was the same expression she'd seen from parents of teenagers after they talked about eye rolling and slamming bedroom doors that came out of seemingly nowhere.

Melody could only guess how much more difficult child-rearing could be when there was only one parent. All the hard decisions fell on one person's shoulders. No one to bounce ideas off of or take some of the heat during an argument.

"Did he quit soccer because of my dad?" Melody asked.

Bebe made a dramatic show of shrugging her shoulders. "Who knows what actually happened to make him quit sports. He came home from school one day and said that he was leaving the team. I never got the real reason out of him. All he said was that he was turning a new page in his life. He'd gotten in a couple of fights at school with his teammates. It's happened before, so I thought it would blow over like always."

"High school can be hard. All those raging hormones and kids being forced in close proximity all the time," Melody sympathized.

"You don't have kids." Bebe's eyebrow arched as she examined Melody.

"No," she admitted. "Afraid I'm not interested in having any, either." She wasn't sure why she felt the need to point that out when her mind had indicated she would consider having a family with someone like Tiernan. The thought shocked her as she forced herself to focus on Bebe. "Why do you ask?"

"You seem to understand a lot about parenting," Bebe said. "More than most single folks."

"I doubt that," she said by way of defense. This wasn't the time to go into how pitiful her personal life had become or the fact there'd been no prospects for a decent date in more months than she cared to count. Annabelle, the administrative assistant from work, would wag her finger at Melody and tell her to go do whatever young people did these days instead of sticking around the office long past closing hours. Melody defended herself by saying she was a career woman. Was that all? Or had her father's action left an indelible mark on her heart? Did he make it impossible to ever trust people, especially men?

"You're welcome to come by the house after work," Bebe said. "I get off in two hours. I wouldn't have come in at all except that I don't have anything else to do with my time now that Jason's gone." Her chin quivered. She blew out a breath. "I can show you pictures and you're welcome to go inside his room. If you want to know who he was."

"I'd like that a lot, actually," Melody said. She glanced over at Tiernan. He'd done so much for her, there was no way she was keeping him from his work the whole day. Plus, the day wasn't turning out like she'd expected. There were other stops needing to be made, too. She could swing by on her own tonight, maybe even bring Loki with her. "Any chance we could come by tonight instead? Maybe bring dinner?"

Bebe smiled but it didn't reach her eyes. "That would be nice."

"Six o'clock okay?" Melody asked.

"Six o'clock," Bebe parroted as Loki came running toward them. "I'd better get back inside. Let me give my number in case you need to get a hold of me."

Melody grabbed her cell phone and entered Bebe's number.

"It's really good to meet you," Melody said when they were finished. "And for what it's worth, I'm sorry about my father."

"He helped make you," Bebe said with a wink. "That means he couldn't have been all bad."

Melody hadn't thought about it that way. She'd put her father on a pedestal until the bubble had burst. And then she'd seen only the worst in him. No one was all bad or good. There had to be layers in between, gray area.

As Bebe walked away, Melody turned toward Tiernan, emotion welling up inside her like a squall. More than anything, she wanted to lean into his comfort and draw from his strength while the storm blew through her. Get lost in him?

For reasons she refused to examine, she walked right up to Tiernan and said, "Where do you stand on kissing?"

Chapter Twelve

Tiernan didn't need a whole lot of convincing to bring his hands up to cup Melody's cheeks and his lips down on hers. The second they touched, a full-fledged fireworks show went off inside his chest. This was the new benchmark for kissing, and he lacked the will to stop. He suspected a wildfire this raging wouldn't come along a whole lot in one lifetime. All he could do at this point was surrender. The damage was going to be vast and deep. He'd deal with the destruction later.

Loki was right beside them, his body against Tiernan's leg. The dog stayed put as Melody's hands came up to brace herself against Tiernan's chest. He dropped his own far enough to take her by the wrists and lower her hands to her sides. Looping his arms around her waist, he pulled her body flush with his. More of those rockets exploded as he splayed his hand on her lower back.

She tasted like honey as he drove his tongue

inside her mouth. He wanted more but this wasn't the place for it. He couldn't stop, either. His heart pounded the inside of his ribs, and it was suddenly like he'd just run a marathon for how intense his breathing had become.

This time, Melody pulled back first. He leaned into her and rested his forehead on hers as he caught his breath. "You're beautiful."

"So are you," she said. The comment made him crack a smile. He found her hand and then walked her over to the passenger side before opening the door. Loki immediately jumped into the back seat of the dual cab.

Tiernan closed the door after Melody claimed her seat. He took his next and she filled him in on her conversation with Bebe.

"I told her we'd be back for dinner, but I know you have work, so I can come on my own," she said.

There was no way in hell that he would stand by and let her take off on her own without him. Not with how wily the sheriff was being with the murder case. Tiernan didn't trust the man as far as he could throw him. Not to mention a killer was still on the loose. "I'll come back with you."

"Are you sure you won't have to work?" she asked. "Because I thought maybe I could bring Loki with me to keep me company on the ride."

"He would like that," he said, touched by the

fact she wanted to spend time with Loki. The two had become fast friends despite her childhood bite experience. Some folks never got over a trauma like that one. The fact they were bonding warmed his heart—a heart that was opening up more and more as he spent time with Melody. "I'd feel a whole lot better if I came with you. Plus, I'd like to learn more about Jason and his mother." He was also thinking of ways he could possibly help her with taking care of her son's burial. "Sounds like she could use a few friends right now."

"I'm sure she would like having you there," Melody said. "I know it would mean a lot to me, too."

Was it a good idea to get this close to Melody? Logic argued against his heart. It wanted to see where this could go. The thought of being away from her caused a foreign ache in his chest. It was probably nothing more than his protective instincts on overdrive.

"Then, I'll figure out the rest," he said, assuming his timelines were short, and he sure didn't want to disappoint a customer. Meeting his deadlines would take some finesse. Everything was doable with the right attitude.

They arrived home in time for a quick lunch of sandwiches and chips, deciding against making a stop to see her father in prison. Melody unpacked in the guest room while he pulled the meal together. By the time she returned, he had food on the table.

She picked up the plates. "No, sir. You don't have time for this." She motioned toward the sliding glass door. "I'll feed you while you work if I have to so you can meet your deadlines."

It had been a long time since someone had taken care of Tiernan. His independent streak was a mile long and Corinne had all but told him that his job was to tend to her. It was a nice change of pace to be with Melody. She had a similar stubborn streak but put others first instead of only thinking about her needs. The proof was in offering to come back to have dinner with Bebe. Melody must have sensed the woman didn't have anyone else. The fact she was at work the day after her only son's body was found spoke a whole lot about her loneliness. His heart went out to the woman. He couldn't imagine loving and protecting someone, from literally helpless infant to a young person full of life ahead and promise, only to have it all cut short. His chest squeezed thinking about the loss, the hurt.

"My workshop is this way," he said to Melody, grabbing keys off the ring before leading the way outside and to the building behind. His pride and joy. He didn't normally lock the door. These were different times.

The workshop was a converted barn, complete with barn doors that slid open. He'd left the metal bar on the outside for show and ambiance. It reminded him of growing up at Hayes Cattle Ranch and his family business. His grandfather might have soured him and his siblings on working there but that didn't mean his childhood on the ranch hadn't been incredible. He'd run around on the property like a wild buck, roaming free on too-hot summer days. Every last one of them worked to keep up the ranch. Duncan Hayes had hired hands once the kids grew up and took off. Now, he was gone and Tiernan was dragging his heels getting home to find out what was on his mother's mind. She'd called a family meeting. He suspected it was to figure out what to do with the business now that Duncan was gone. A conversation no one had wanted to have.

At this point, half of them had gone back. He wasn't ready. His own business had been as good excuse as any.

"This place is impressive," Melody said as her gaze roamed over the big open space after he flipped on the lights. A hydraulic press took up what used to be a stall. "You'll have to walk me through how you make one of those after you get caught up." She nodded toward the desk on the left side of the room. "Is that where I should set down our plates?"

"Sure," he said, closing the door behind them. Loki ran around the room with his usual excitement. He had a bed to one side of the room along with a few toys in a basket, not that they stayed there much. He couldn't count the number of times he'd stepped on a squeaky toy. The tile flooring made for easy cleanup when Loki knocked over food or water bowls, which happened more than Tiernan wanted to admit.

As Melody set up at the desk, he grabbed an extra stool.

"I just keep thinking about Bebe," Melody said as she sat down. Loki came rushing over, sat down next to her and looked up at her with the biggest pair of sad brown eyes.

"Don't fall for it," Tiernan warned. "Dogs have the ability to whip out their 'puppy eyes' when they want table scraps. Trust me, he goes back to being his normal self when the food is eaten or put away."

"He is looking extra cute right now," she said with a smile. "Is he allowed to have one bite or is the plate off limits?"

Tiernan would feel like a complete jerk for being the reason Loki lost out on a sliver of turkey and cheese.

Before he could respond, a clicking sound

from the door area caught Loki's interest. He hopped up and bolted toward the noise. Melody's face twisted with concern as Tiernan held up a finger to indicate she should sit tight for a second while he checked it out.

A sound like a hammer splintering wood repeated several times as though someone was running around the building. Tiernan bolted toward the door and tried to slide it open. He bit back a string of curses that would make Granny blush when it wouldn't budge.

Tiernan threw his shoulder into it as Loki started running around the perimeter of the former barn. A window broke and was immediately followed by the stench of smoke.

Bottle after bottle exploded through windows as fire broke out in the shop.

MELODY JUMPED TO her feet. She'd seen a fire extinguisher attached to a support pole. "Is this thing up to code?"

"It came with the building," he said, already running toward another one. "Considering these are our best hope, we can't be too picky."

"How flammable is the barn?" she asked, wondering just how much time she had left to live as she ran toward the wall. The bottles crashing reminded her of the Molotov cocktails she'd seen in old movies.

She pulled her shirt up over her mouth and nose. At this rate, smoke would fill the room and they'd die from inhalation before the fire ever got to them. Her brain snapped to Loki, and there was no way in hell she planned to let that happen to him. She jerked the red canister off the wooden pole. "What do I do?"

"Pull the pin, aim and squeeze the trigger," he said as he did the same as he checked his gauge and cursed. He said the same word she was thinking. "Mine has no pressure."

She checked hers.

"Mine's low, but there's something here," she said. "Take it and I'll call 911."

They made the exchange but not before he tested his out. The pressure gauge was on the money. There was not enough.

She immediately grabbed his cell phone and made the call for help.

"The operator says it'll take fifteen minutes for the closest volunteer firefighter to reach us," she said, knowing full well an entire house could go up in a matter of minutes. She glanced around for anything she could use to slow the progression of the fire. There was a sink in one corner that might help if it worked. She grabbed a pair of buckets that were hanging on the wall, no doubt leftovers from the original barn.

Filling the buckets, she ran over to the left

wall and threw the water in an attempt to douse the flames. Loki was going crazy at this point. The air was getting thicker by the minute.

"We can't wait to get out of here," Tiernan said. "We're going to have to break out through the wall." He ran over and grabbed the metal stool that he'd been sitting on a few minutes ago.

A few seconds later, he was using the stool like a battering ram against the wooden wall. She joined him, using a long, metal tool. She had no idea what it was and didn't care at the moment. With all her might, she pounded the wood. Between the two of them, they started making progress.

When there was enough give in the wood, Tiernan threw his shoulder into it repeatedly as both began to cough. One last burst, and the wood exploded. Tiernan went flying onto the grass outside. Loki immediately followed, but he caught sight of something or someone and tore off in a different direction.

"Loki, no!" Melody shouted but the dog was locked on to something. Tiernan had already jumped to his feet, scanning the area no doubt for something he could use to put out the blaze. A water hose would be like bringing a straw to an ocean to drain it.

"Don't let your guard down," he said to her as he ran to the house. He retrieved a pair of working fire extinguishers and handed one over as he yelled for Loki. "We won't have enough juice to put out the blaze with these but maybe we can slow the fire down enough until help arrives to be able to salvage something."

She nodded before pulling the pin. *Aim and squeeze.*

Loki was still gone when the fire truck arrived. Half the building was standing. The contents had to be ruined either by fire, extinguisher, or water damage. Tiernan looked gutted at the damage to a business he deeply cared about.

Panic gripped her at what could have happened. That wasn't just a close call. That could have been certain death. The person who set the fires knew they were inside. Had they been watching? Waiting?

The sheriff would have to believe her now. Have to take her off the suspect list. It dawned on her that she needed to call Bebe to cancel their dinner plans. Melody hated to do it but she had no other choice. They would need to stick around to give statements and find Loki.

Ice ran through her veins at the thought someone wanted her dead. Because of her, Tiernan could have been killed and Loki was missing. She had to face the fact it might not be good for Tiernan's longevity if she stuck around. The idea of anything happening to him was worse than her being murdered.

She lived alone and had very few friends. She'd distanced herself from a dysfunctional family. She wasn't close to anyone at the office. Would anyone even miss her?

The answer was sobering.

"I have to find him," Tiernan said to her, breaking through her heavy thoughts. "Can you handle things here?"

"Yes. Go," she said, praying he could find him and wishing she could go with him to hunt for the dog who'd made his way into her heart.

In a surprising move, Tiernan dipped his head down and kissed her before taking off in the direction Loki had gone.

Melody figured this was as good a time as any to reach out to Bebe. She retrieved her cell phone, which thankfully had survived along with her handbag that was wet but okay, and made the call.

"Hello?" Bebe sounded unsure if it was a good idea to answer.

"Hi, it's Melody," she said.

"Oh, Melody," Bebe repeated the name.

"Everything all right?" Melody asked. She didn't like how shaken Bebe sounded.

"Yes. Fine," Bebe said. "What's up?"

Melody didn't want to worry Bebe but she

didn't want her to think they were blowing her off. "There's been an incident at Tiernan's house and we need to stay in tonight to deal with it."

"Nothing bad I hope." Bebe's tone raised with concern and a defensiveness that said she couldn't take much more bad news.

"An accident happened in the workshop," she reassured. "I'd still like to come for dinner. Maybe tomorrow night? Would that work?"

"Sure," Bebe said with a twinge of disappointment in her voice. The loneliness must be almost unbearable. Melody's heart nearly cracked in two. "Do what you need to. I'll be around."

"Is it okay if I reach out later once we get this all sorted out?" Melody asked.

"Sure is," Bebe said, a little more reassured-sounding now.

The fire didn't take long to put out with the proper equipment.

"Fire Marshal is on his way," one of the firemen said. "I'm Jerome, by the way."

"Melody," she said as he tipped his chin in acknowledgment. "What about the sheriff?"

Jerome shrugged. He wasn't nearly as tall as Tiernan. Jerome was thick. Thick hands. Thick neck. Thick arms. Stocky would be a better term to use to describe him. The two-man team had stood rooted to their spots as they'd sprayed chemicals to put out the fire.

"All I know is the marshal wants us to be careful now that the blaze is out, so we don't trample all over possible evidence. Basically, this is being treated as an arson case."

A yelp echoed through the night.

Loki.

Chapter Thirteen

Loki was in trouble. Tiernan had heard the same sound coming from his dog when he'd got himself tangled up in barbed wire on the neighbor's property. The panicked yelp cut right through Tiernan's chest. He pivoted toward the sound and pushed his legs until his thighs burned. Branches slapped him in the face as he zigzagged through the trees.

The toe of his boot caught on scrub brush, causing him to take a couple of giant steps forward and ending with him face-planting into a tree trunk. Arm out in front, he managed to minimize the impact and come up with only a couple of new scratches and—thankfully—no brain damage. Something cold and wet dripped into his eyes. His first thought was sweat. As he wiped away the moisture, he realized it was blood. Not great but not enough to stop him, either.

Calling out to the dog would be a mistake in the event the person who'd set the fire had Loki.

Not a thought Tiernan was thrilled about but he had to consider the possibility. Alerting the bastard to Tiernan's presence would take away the element of surprise and put him at a severe disadvantage.

With any luck—not something Tiernan could rely on considering he'd gotten where he was today by hard work and *not* relying on chance— Loki had stepped on something and that was the cause for the distress call. There were wild boars in these parts along with other animals, predators.

Chest pounding, pulse jacked up to the sky, Tiernan tried to breathe through a burst of adrenaline. In another minute, his sensory overload would settle, and his thoughts would be crystal clear until the boost wore off.

Another yelp from Loki didn't help matters. Tiernan muttered a curse and shifted direction a little more east. He knew this property like the back of his hand, which should provide some advantage.

Loki started rapid-fire barking now, making it easier to home in on his location. Had he freed himself from something or someone? An animal?

Nearing the sound, Tiernan slowed his pace. The moon provided enough light to see now that his eyes had adjusted to the darkness—darkness that came early in the winter. The scratch on his forehead was bleeding, not exactly a sieve but not a dribble. Foreheads were bleeders. He could assess the damage once he got back to the house.

The barking stopped, and then a moment later Tiernan heard heavy breathing. The black Lab burst from behind a tree in full-on get-the-hell-out-of-Dodge mode.

"Loki, sit," Tiernan said with authority. The dog was too wound up to listen, but something might register.

Loki blasted past and then seemed to have a second thought when he looked left to right and slowed his pace.

"Loki," Tiernan repeated.

The dog made an about-face so fast he was almost a blur. Tiernan kept an eye out in the direction from which Loki came just in case something or someone followed.

Rather than wait for Loki to double back, Tiernan turned toward home and ran while urging his buddy to follow. Sticking around out here wouldn't do either one of them any good. The sheriff and his deputies could search the property in case the arsonist tried to escape this way.

At this point, Tiernan had half a mind to nominate Loki for search and rescue. It might be a good way to put his highly sensitive sense of smell to use. Then again, working dogs had high stress and Loki deserved pampering.

Tiernan turned an ear toward the trail behind them, on alert to see if they were being followed. So far, so good. But he wouldn't take anything for granted.

MELODY PACED THE length of the cabin as she waited for the sheriff to input his report into the laptop mounted on his dashboard. She'd gone over the details of what had happened despite wishing she was out there, searching for Loki beside Tiernan. She second-guessed agreeing to stay back and deal with the law. The sheriff had taken notes. He'd nodded at all the appropriate times. So, why was she convinced that he didn't believe her?

Tiernan would corroborate her story when he returned with Loki, which was the only scenario she could allow herself to consider. Her brain couldn't accept any other outcome. Hope was all she had at this point, and she intended to hold on to it like a child's hand as she crossed a busy street.

The deputy walked around, gathering evidence and taking pictures from various angles. The evidence would fall in line with her statement. No question there. Then, it occurred to her that she should have called Prescott before giving her statement.

Melody palmed her cell, figuring better late than never. He picked up on the first ring.

"There's been an incident at the house." She

went right into it. "A fire in Tiernan's workshop while we were inside. Someone barricaded us in."

"Is the sheriff there?" Prescott immediately asked.

"Yes. I've just given a statement," she said. "I could be wrong but it didn't seem like he believed me."

"If he asks you any more questions, refer him to me," Prescott said. "Where's Tiernan?"

"He went to follow Loki after he ran off," she said, hearing the shakiness in her own voice. The thought of anything happening to either one of them gutted her.

"Has he spoken to the sheriff?" Prescott asked.

"Not yet," she said, then hesitated before asking the question that was simmering in the back of her mind. "Would it be possible for me to be placed somewhere safe while we sort all this out? I can't go home and there's no one else that I trust."

Prescott seemed like he needed a minute to process her request and all the implications that came along with it. "May I ask why?"

"Yes," she said. "I'd like to leave Tiernan out of this."

"I understand," Prescott said. "Could I offer a few thoughts?"

"Okay," she said but doubted there was anything he could say to change her mind. She needed to spend a couple of days in a safe house so she could gather her thoughts and figure out her next move. Involving Tiernan further only put him in more danger.

"Tiernan Hayes is a big boy," Prescott started. "He wouldn't be here if he didn't want to be."

"Understood," she said. Before she could come up with an argument, the lawyer continued.

"He is already involved," he said. "The person who set the fire was going after Tiernan, as well. This has now become personal for him since the perp brought the fight to his doorstep, twice now."

She bit her bottom lip rather than mount another argument.

"You can leave him but that doesn't make him safer, because he'll go after the perp full throttle," Prescott said. His logic made more sense than she wanted it to. "If you stay put, it'll help me contain him so he doesn't end up in real trouble. As long as you're there, he won't take unnecessary risks."

"You make it sound like he would go rogue and do something stupid," she said. "If there's one thing I know about Tiernan it's that he's smart."

"I'm not suggesting otherwise," Prescott said. "But he could turn reckless in his pursuit of the perp, and everyone involved will be a lot better off if he lets me do my job."

Before Melody could respond, Prescott redirected the conversation. "The handwriting on the note found on your vehicle and the one in the victim's pocket match. They have a handwriting expert taking a look at the evidence."

"It's creepy but maybe this will help move the investigation in a better direction," she said.

"We can hope, but I wouldn't relax just yet," Prescott warned. "The sheriff is requesting a handwriting sample from you."

"To clear my name?" she asked.

"Or to prove his case," Prescott said.

There was no way that would happen because she didn't write either note.

Melody issued a sharp sigh as a dark figure emerged from the trees. Correction, *two* figures were running full force. Her heart would sing if it could hold a note.

"He's here. Loki's fine. I'll call you back," she said to Prescott as she cut across the lawn, running toward them. As Loki neared, she dropped down to her knees while tears streaked her cheeks.

The Lab bowled her over. She collapsed onto her side as Loki dropped his head down in dog pose. The sight of Tiernan must be what people meant when they described what heaven on earth looked like. Her heart nearly exploded in her chest as the tension she didn't realize she'd been holding released as though a dam broke and floodgates opened.

By the time Tiernan reached her, she was sitting up and hugging Loki. His fur was slick with—she checked her hands—blood.

Sheer panic replaced calm as Tiernan reached her. A gash on his forehead was pulsing blood. Their gazes locked for a couple of seconds as he took a knee. The worry in his beautiful eyes for Loki while Tiernan was clearly in need of medical assistance himself tugged at her heartstrings.

"What happened?" she asked, studying his gash. "You're hurt."

"I'm not worried about me right now," he said. "It's probably just a scratch."

She bit her tongue because Tiernan wouldn't listen, not right now, not while he was intent on making sure Loki would be okay.

It took a few minutes, but Tiernan was finally able to calm Loki down enough to run his hand over the dog's head and torso. Loki whimpered when Tiernan's hand reached his right hindquarter.

"I think I just found the problem," Tiernan said. In the next few seconds, his T-shirt was off and he was using it to stem Loki's bleeding while offering quiet reassurances that were working.

Panting on his side, Loki lay flat against the grass. As Tiernan calmed him, Melody found the fireman from a little while ago and asked if he had an emergency medical kit.

"Yes, ma'am," Jerome said before jogging over to his truck. He followed her over to Tiernan. "That's a big cut on your forehead, sir. Mind if I take a look?"

Before Tiernan could dismiss the offer, Melody said, "I'll watch Loki." She sat near the Lab's head and stroked him behind the ears.

Jerome hollered at someone to bring a bowl of water for Loki before going to work patching up Tiernan's forehead. By the time Jerome had cleaned the wound and put antibiotic ointment on it, Loki was lapping up bottled water being poured into another one of the firemen's hands.

"You're going to be all right, little buddy," the fireman said. There was something special about dog lovers. The way they all pitched in to care for strays or dogs belonging to others. She'd seen people stop traffic to help out a lost dog. Restaurants in downtown Austin put bowls in front of their establishments with fresh water for passersby. Dog lovers were a community unto their own.

Before she could give Tiernan an update, an all-black sporty Mercedes-Benz wheeled into the drive, kicking up a dust storm in the process. Through the cloud emerged Prescott, wearing jeans and a hand-tailored black button-down shirt. He walked with purpose straight to the sheriff's vehicle.

"Our job here is done when the lawyers show up," Jerome said on a chuckle.

"Thank you for everything," Melody said, stopping short of giving the man a hug out of gratitude.

"All in a day's work," Jerome said before he and his buddy headed back toward their vehicle, stopping off at the sheriff's SUV first.

Looking at Tiernan now, she realized Prescott was right. If she took off now, Tiernan wouldn't stop until he found the person or persons responsible for the fire and for hurting his beloved Loki. Her leaving would only make matters worse. Tiernan might take more risks, as the lawyer had pointed out.

Seeing how protective his nature was didn't help her keep an emotional distance from the man. She would have to try harder or risk losing her heart.

Prescott finished with the sheriff, then headed straight toward them. Tiernan reached for her hand but she moved it in time to avoid contact. The less their skin touched, the better as far as she was concerned.

The hurt look on his face almost gutted her. The serious expression on the lawyer's face said bad news was coming their way.

Chapter Fourteen

"The sheriff is off his rocker," Prescott started in while Tiernan double-checked Loki's wound. The bleeding had stopped. A good sign. Still, he needed to get to the vet as soon as possible.

"What does that mean exactly?" Tiernan asked. Melody's rejection from a minute ago had bruised his ego. He told himself it was for the best. As it was, he was falling down a slippery slope when it came to how he felt about her. The wall she'd put up between them was a good reminder not to get too close.

"This is clearly an arson case," Prescott said. "There's no way either of you would do this on purpose to detract attention from Melody as a possible murder suspect."

"He said that?" Tiernan asked, furious. "Because that means he's questioning my honor."

"Not in exactly those words," Prescott stated. "I told him that I expect a copy of his report on my desk by morning or that I'd be calling in experts to review the evidence on my own."

"What did he say to that?" Melody chimed in.

"That I wasn't allowed to tamper with his crime scene," Prescott said.

"What right does he have to insinuate something like that?" she continued.

"None," Prescott said. "But this is a small town and he probably has Sunday night poker with the local judge. Which is why I'd file for a change in venue for a trial if he does a stupid thing and arrests you."

Melody gasped and her eyes widened.

"They'd have to take me in, too," Tiernan said, meaning every word.

"I think he's prepared to do that if he goes down that route," Prescott said. "Make arrangements for Loki just in case. Okay?"

Tiernan nodded.

"Does that mean I'd spend time in jail?" Melody asked, clearly mortified.

"Not more than a couple of hours," Prescott said. "I would immediately file a motion to relocate the case to Austin where you'd get a fair jury pull and trial. If the sheriff is making a move like this with me, his confidence tells me something. He must think he has this thing in the bag."

"That doesn't sound good," Melody continued, staring up at the vast evening sky. There was a chill in the air and she'd started shivering. His shirt was bloody or he'd hand it over.

"Can we move this inside?" he asked Prescott. "Loki will do better indoors. Plus, your client is cold."

Prescott nodded. "Of course. My apologies."

Tiernan scooped up the seventy-five-pound Lab and carried him to his bed on the floor in the dining room. "I need to get a vet over here now. Mind if I make a quick call?"

"Go right ahead," Prescott said. He palmed his cell phone and started firing off a bunch of texts, no doubt to the investigators he'd already hired to look into the case.

"I'll put on coffee," Melody said, looking like she needed something to do more so than a caffeine boost. Her hands already trembled. Then again, she might want the warmth.

While on the call to his vet, Tiernan retrieved one of his jackets from the closet and brought it over to her as she stood at the coffee machine. He draped it around her shoulders.

She thanked him without making eye contact. The shivering stopped, though, so he'd take the win.

Prescott tucked his phone inside his pocket as he joined them in the kitchen. "Is there another place you can stay besides here?"

"My apartment is a terrible idea," Melody said. Her ringtone sounded. She fished her cell out of her back pocket. "My mother?"

Tiernan knew the two weren't close. The call seemed to catch her off guard.

"Do you mind if I take this?" she asked, looking at Prescott.

"Go ahead," he said. "Tiernan can bring you up to date if you miss anything."

"Hello?" Melody answered after a quick nod. Nervous tension pulled her shoulders taut. Concern lines scored her forehead. She rolled her head around like she was trying to ease some of the knots.

He turned to Prescott with an ear toward Melody.

"Coffee?" he asked the lawyer.

"Yes, please," Prescott said. The move also stalled for time since he wanted to hear at least Melody's side of the conversation with her mother. He grabbed mugs and began pouring, hearing a few starts and stops coming from Melody as she kept getting cut off.

"So, you're worried about Coop and that's the reason for the call?" Melody asked, indignant. She muttered a few words that he couldn't make out as Prescott took one of the mugs on the counter.

Tiernan motioned toward the dining table where he brought the other two.

"I'm sorry you don't think I'm 'there' enough for you and Coop, but you two aren't the only ones going through this and..." Melody must have gotten cut off. She issued a sigh. "What? When?"

The concern in her voice drew the lawyer's attention, as well.

"What was stolen?" she asked. A few beats of silence passed as Melody chewed on her bottom lip. He liked the look of his jacket around her shoulders more than he wanted to admit. But he was concerned about the conversation. "What else?" The blood drained from Melody's face, turning it bleached-sheet white. She glanced over at him and mouthed, *a locket.*

Tiernan cursed. Prescott nodded. He got it. The locket that had been dropped off at his office belonged to Melody's mother.

"The blood on the locket is a match to Jason's," Prescott informed. "My guess is that someone intended to plant it at your home."

Melody brought her hand up to cover a gasp, muting the mic. "It would tie me to Jason's murder."

"The sheriff said he had an informant who pointed the finger at you," Prescott said. "But he didn't produce a name."

"Because he doesn't have one?" she asked.

"That's my guess," Prescott stated. "The sheriff is stalling."

"How did the person break in?" Melody asked after rejoining the conversation with her mother. She was quiet for a long moment. "I'm sorry this happened to you." She paused. "I'm sure Coop is out of his mind with worry. Is he going to stay with you?" Another beat passed. "I'm sure he's too busy." Silence. "No. I didn't mean anything by it. Coop is a busy person." The unspoken words were *unlike me*. "I'm sure he is doing everything he can." More of that silence came. "I'll check on you, Mom. Don't worry about me. I'm good." The words had a slight chill to them. "Talk to you later."

Her mother didn't ask how her daughter was doing?

Melody ended the call and then joined them at the table. "Sorry about that."

"No need to apologize," he said quickly. "Sounds like we solved the mystery of where the locket came from."

"My mother's house was broken into five days ago, but she didn't discover the break-in or the missing locket until yesterday," Melody supplied. "Her housekeeper figured it out and put a timeline together."

"Your mom doesn't have any camera security?" Prescott asked.

Melody shook her head. "She decided the government is keeping an eye on everyone through their own security devices. She's paranoid about being watched and doesn't want to make it any easier on them than it already is. She went on a rant about how we're all giving up way too much information about ourselves with all these devices."

Tiernan didn't use much more than a cell and a laptop. His social media was nonexistent except for his business account. For him, it was less about privacy and more about being too busy to fiddle with it. Plus, the last thing he wanted to do was stare at a screen all day. Speaking of his business, he needed to make a whole lot of phone calls to let customers know their orders were no longer possible by Christmas.

Prescott was making notes in his phone.

"Do you have a key to your mother's place?" he asked.

"No," she said after a thoughtful pause. "Not since she moved out of our family home."

"Where did the break-in occur?" Prescott asked.

Tiernan knew exactly where the lawyer was going with this line of questioning. He was assessing the risk of the sheriff accusing Melody of the crime.

MELODY GRIPPED THE warm mug, rolling it between her palms. Someone broke into her mother's place and stole a locket. "Kitchen window is where he got it. Don't you think this makes it look like someone bent on revenge is behind the crime?"

"It's a possibility," Tiernan said quickly.

"Jason was an illegitimate son who didn't get his due after contacting my father," she reasoned out loud. "There could be others out there."

"True," Prescott said. "Your father had a history of infidelity."

It was an honest statement.

"That's right," Melody said, ignoring the pain in her chest at the admission. She might know who and what her father was, but that didn't make it sting any less every time the subject came up. "We have no idea if he had more children."

"There was you, your brother and the victim," Prescott said.

"The setup makes it look like Jason was jealous and that's the reason he was coming for you," Tiernan said.

"It doesn't quite scan for me, though," Melody said.

"I tend to agree," Tiernan stated.

"Going over to Bebe's place for dinner tonight would most likely help us get a better sense of the kid," she continued. "His bedroom will reveal a lot about him and his character."

Prescott raised an eyebrow, so she explained the trip they'd made to the grocer earlier. He frowned two seconds into the account.

"No more visiting potential witnesses," Prescott said sternly. "Understood?"

"Melody had questions about her half-brother," Tiernan defended.

"Maybe so," Prescott said. "And they weren't out of line except that we have a serious case on our hands and the sheriff is rooting around in the wrong direction. I just don't need him tying anything else back to you. It doesn't seem to matter how loose the tether is, he is looking for ways to implicate you."

Melody nodded as a liquid fireball shot through her veins. "What is it with this guy? Why is he locking on to me?"

"Good questions," Prescott said. "I suspect you're an easy target and the guy isn't exactly good at his job."

"What if it's more?" Tiernan cut in. "What if he has a thing against women?"

"My guess is the guy figures everyone in the Cantor family is a criminal at this point," Prescott said. "The law enforcement axiom, 'The easy answer is usually the right one,' applies in this case. Her being jealous of an illegitimate brother who might be stepping in to try and take away inheritance could be a motive for murder. She could be protecting her father if the kid threatened to call the media and claim his birthright."

"Wouldn't it make more sense for my brother to be the one to have…" She couldn't say the words *killed Jason*. They were too heinous, and she didn't want to believe there was even the slightest possibility her brother could be capable of murder.

"Yes," Prescott said. "Keep in mind, he has an ironclad alibi."

"Right, the trip," she said. "He wouldn't have been in town at the time of Jason's death."

"And this has been verified six ways past Tuesday?" Tiernan asked.

"As much as possible," Prescott said.

"What about the break-in?" Melody asked. "My father has a lot of enemies, and there is a strong possibility that someone might be targeting my family."

"The sheriff doesn't want to see it that way," Prescott said. "This case could turn political in a heartbeat." It dawned on her this could be the reason Prescott had taken the case in the first place. A man of his stature wouldn't normally take on a small-time client, even with a recommendation from a family as powerful as Tiernan's. Prescott saw two steps down the road and the potential for a political hotbed. Otherwise, he probably would have handed this off to a junior associate in his firm.

"I have what I need for now," Prescott said as he closed his small laptop. "If the sheriff contacts you or, heaven forbid, goes for an arrest, call me immediately."

"Will do," Tiernan said as Melody tried to process this reality. The one involving her being locked behind bars.

Tiernan walked Prescott to the front door, then locked it behind him before checking his cell phone after a message came in. "We'll figure this out before it comes to being arrested."

"I sure hope so." Melody needed to speak to her brother in person in order to judge whether or not Coop could possibly have any involvement, and the conversation couldn't wait.

Chapter Fifteen

"I need to go see Coop right now." The stern quality to Melody's voice told Tiernan she wouldn't be talked out of the idea easily.

"The sheriff might be there right now," he pointed out. "The last thing we need is to run into him."

Melody crossed her arms over her chest, ready to defend her argument. "I will be able to tell if my brother is lying. They won't."

Tiernan glanced at the clock. "It's getting late. We need to grab a bite to eat and turn in early. The vet got sidetracked but he'll be here in a few minutes. Why not take a shower while I make sure Loki is fine?"

Her gaze swung over to the sleeping dog.

"Loki," she said under her breath. "I got so wrapped up in my own problem that I forgot how much he must be suffering." The disgust in her voice was misguided at best. She didn't need to be so hard on herself.

"He's resting, which is an encouraging sign," he reassured. "Believe me, if I thought he was in bad shape, he'd already be at an animal hospital and not resting in his own bed. At this point, the vet visit is just to make sure he doesn't end up with a secondary infection and to dot every *i* and cross every *t*. I don't take chances where his health is concerned."

She nodded and gave a look of respect and appreciation that melted some of Tiernan's resolve to keep her at arm's length. He didn't need a whole lot of encouragement to go there with her.

"I could use a shower," she said after a thoughtful pause. She knelt down beside Loki and stroked his neck. "You're going to be just fine." She said the words quietly. "You are such a brave boy."

"Go get cleaned up," Tiernan urged, figuring he hadn't met a day so awful that a good shower couldn't wash it off. Watching her there with Loki put an unfamiliar ache in his chest. The twinge had him thinking about marriage and children, despite the promises he'd made to himself not to fall for anyone again after Corinne. His judgment had been so far off with her that he'd missed the target altogether. How could he trust that he wasn't falling into the same trap here? He'd known Melody Cantor all of a couple of days. Not enough time to really get to know someone. He'd rushed into a relationship with Corinne. Look how that had turned out. She'd tried to break his reputation and destroy him.

Still, when Melody looked up at him with eyes that resembled spun gold, all he could think of was figuring out how to claim those pink lips of hers and walk away with his heart intact.

He moved closer and offered a hand up, ignoring the electricity charging the air when he got within two feet of Melody. At this point, he was getting used to it. Welcoming it?

"The vet is on his way. Take your time in the shower. Once you're done, I'll heat food and we'll be set for the night," he said, doing his level best not to give in to the urge to kiss her. A place he usually kept locked up. Corinne hadn't come anywhere close, and he'd foolishly believed he was in love with her at one point in time.

Melody let go of his hand, excused herself and walked toward the guest room as his cell phone buzzed. He walked over to the counter where he'd left it and checked the screen. Outside, he could hear tires on gravel. Dr. Paul Macy was here.

Tiernan headed toward the front door. The vet had the good sense to text rather than ring a doorbell or knock, knowing an injured dog would still likely run to the door and bark at the noise. Tiernan opened the door and waited for Dr. Paul.

"How is he?" Dr. Paul asked after parking near the front porch and exiting his F-150. He had a medical bag in his left hand.

"I don't think he's as badly injured as I initially believed," Tiernan said. "I'd still like you to give him a good once-over just to make sure."

Loki limped up to Tiernan and the vet.

"Hey, Loki," Dr. Paul said, bending down to eye level with the black Lab. He reached into his pocket and pulled out a stinky treat. The man always smelled like liver bits, which was probably the reason dogs loved him. "Let's go inside and have a look at you."

Tiernan took a step back and held out his hand for the vet to enter. "Where do you want him?"

"Anywhere he will be comfortable is fine," Dr. Paul said, leading the way to Loki's bed in the dining room.

"I appreciate you coming on such short notice," Tiernan said.

Dr. Paul gave a smile and a nod. "What happened to your workshop?"

The burnt smell was still in the air outside, Tiernan had noticed after opening the front door.

"Arson," Tiernan answered honestly.

"I'm sorry to hear it," Dr. Paul said as he set down his bag and then made himself comfortable on the floor. Loki complied with lying down, considering there was another treat involved. "Was Loki around when it happened?"

"He was inside the building with us," Tiernan said, motioning toward the guest room so Dr. Paul wasn't caught off guard when Melody came out if he was still around. Chances were that he would be. Tiernan hadn't had anyone over in a long time.

"I'll check his lungs," Dr. Paul said with a frown. "It might be a good idea for me to take him into the clinic overnight so I can give him oxygen just to be safe."

"Whatever you need to do," Tiernan said.

"He's young and strong," Dr. Paul reassured. He must have heard the slight note of panic in Tiernan's voice. "His cuts aren't very deep, so that's good. Although, I do need to deal with them. Wouldn't want to risk infection."

"He's been to your clinic before," Tiernan said. "He'll be comfortable there."

"I'll stay with him overnight to make certain," Dr. Paul promised.

There were no words for the appreciation Tiernan felt for Dr. Paul and his quality of care. He offered a handshake as the vet stood.

"What do you need help with?" Tiernan asked.

"I'll grab the stretcher from the truck," he said

before heading out the front. He returned a few moments later with stretcher in hand.

With Tiernan's help, Loki was inside the truck curled in a ball within a couple of minutes. A knot lodged in Tiernan's throat as Dr. Paul pulled away. The thought of something bad happening to his own kids someday nearly gutted him.

The walk to the living room was slow. He needed to get on his laptop after dinner so he could update his clients on the status of their orders. Like it or not, Christmas was coming with the speed of a roaring freight train. If someone had told him that he would be in the thick of a murder investigation right now he wouldn't have believed them.

Tiernan moved into the kitchen and heated a couple of plates of food before setting them on the granite island. As he turned around, he stepped on one of Loki's squeaky toys. Tiernan wasn't big on displays of emotion, but the reminder caused a squall to rise up in his chest. His ribs squeezed around his heart to the point he had to take a couple of slow, deep breaths to right himself again.

"Everything okay?" Melody asked as she walked into the room. He'd seen her out of the corner of his eye. She glanced around the room and her face dropped. "Where's Loki?"

MELODY'S HEART WENT out to Tiernan the second she saw the look on his face when she entered the living area. There was an indescribable emptiness in the space now, which was strange considering she'd never owned a pet. She could barely keep a plant alive. It was good to know herself. No innocent lives died due to her neglect.

"Dr. Paul took him to his clinic," Tiernan said, his voice rough. He cleared his throat, no doubt trying to cover.

"Why?" she asked.

He gave the quick rundown.

"Sounds like it's better to be safe than sorry," she said, trying to offer some reassurance.

He motioned toward their plates that were filled with rib eye steaks, spinach and baked potatoes. At home, Melody usually ate a TV dinner before bed. Eating here reminded her of everything she was missing in homemade meals. Granted, the ready-made ones were decently edible. This was on another level.

Melody took her seat and then started eating. Tiernan grabbed his laptop.

"There are two plates here," she said, hoping he would join her.

He nodded.

"You forced me to shower a little bit ago and it made a huge difference," she said. "I hope you'll let me return the favor by pressuring you to eat."

Tiernan stared at her for a long moment, indecision written all over his features.

"Please," she said.

Her plea worked because he walked over and sat down next to her. She reached over and touched his forearm.

"For what it's worth, I'm sorry," she said.

Tiernan's muscles tensed. "It's not your fault."

"It feels like it might be," she said. "I came into your life and look what's happened."

"Don't do that to yourself," he countered. "Don't blame yourself for things outside your control. You didn't ask for any of this, either. Bad things happen to good people."

He was making sense. And yet, guilt still slammed into her at the thought Loki was in a clinic tonight rather than home in his bed. If she'd left last night, would the fire have happened?

"Still," she said.

"The body was found on my property," Tiernan said after finishing a bite. "That couldn't possibly be your fault. You've been dragged into this as much as I have. Neither of us is to blame for the events unfolding."

"Tell the sheriff that," she quipped.

"He's a jerk and clearly not qualified to lead an investigation," Tiernan said.

Melody finished another bite. "No argument there."

The rest of the meal was spent in companionable silence. When the plates were cleared and cleaned, Melody poured two glasses of water. She held one up for Tiernan, who took the offering. He downed the contents in a matter of seconds.

"I think I'm going to grab a shower before I reach out to my clients," he said. The image of him naked wasn't something she needed stuck in her thoughts.

She glanced around, realizing she would be alone in the room. He must have picked up on her hesitation because he grabbed her by the hand and then linked their fingers as he walked them into the primary bedroom.

The room was a good size. A king bed was anchored against one wall. The headboard looked hand carved from oak. It was beautiful. There was a dresser along with a pair of coordinating nightstands. Blinds covered the windows—windows she was certain looked onto the backyard and now burned-down workshop. Her heart still hurt that he'd lost everything he'd worked so hard for. She did realize insurance would cover the cost to rebuild. But what about all that lost revenue from clients?

"I'll leave the door cracked in case you need to shout for me," he said as he walked her over to his bed. The mattress was set high, so she practically had to climb to sit on it. "What can I get you to make you more comfortable?"

"Honestly, I'm good," she said. "Okay if I lean back and rest my eyes?"

"Go for it," he said before disappearing into the adjacent bathroom. As promised, he left the door cracked enough to keep her pulse from racing. She didn't realize how much she'd come to depend on having another living being in the room until now. Having Loki around was nice. Maybe when this ordeal was over, she would get a pet. Cats were supposed to be low maintenance. Melody also needed to get a job once she got past this case. She *would* get beyond this. Right? The thought of being sent to prison was enough to send an icy chill racing down her spine. Not to mention being locked up for a crime she didn't commit. Her thoughts shifted to Bebe. No mother should have to endure losing a child, least of all one so young. It was unimaginable. Melody shook her head at the carnage her father had left behind. How did she ever love the man?

Innocence, she thought. She'd been someone who believed in family and loved her father blindly. Melody issued a sharp sigh. The worst part was not wanting to hate her father. There were times when she wished she could go back to her young and naive self. The one who believed the world was made up of rainbows and butterflies.

Then again, maybe going into a situation with eyes wide open was a good thing. Plus, she would never allow anyone close enough to hurt her again. Her own family had proved those closest had the power to cut the deepest.

Melody propped up a couple of pillows on the massive bed. This had to be bigger than a king. Custom order? Tiernan was a big guy, tall with lean muscles—muscles she didn't want to think about while she was lying on top of his bed and breathing in his spicy scent from the pillows.

It would be so easy to lean in to her attraction to him. And then what? She was facing possible jail time for a crime she didn't commit. Could she use a friend right now? The answer was a hard yes. She was still racking her brain trying to figure out who could have robbed her mother, stolen the locket and then placed it on her doorstep. What about the blood? Her skin crawled just thinking about it belonging to a half-brother she never got the chance to meet.

Her mother's call from earlier was eating away at Melody, too. Her mother might not know the situation Melody was in, but the woman didn't ask questions. She never once asked if Melody was all right or if she needed anything. Her mother called to have someone to complain to or fish for pity, sometimes both. And, plus, why was Melody just now being told about the break-in?

Melody's head hurt thinking about all this. And so did her heart.

Chapter Sixteen

Tiernan showered, dried off and threw on boxers, and then stepped into his room to find Melody asleep on his bed. His chest tightened at the sleeping image of her. Long russet locks splayed on his pillow. She was curled on her side, half sitting up. This whole scenario looked a little too right.

He moved into the kitchen to retrieve his laptop. Since she didn't want to be alone, he returned to the bedroom and set the device on the chair next to the bed.

Gingerly, he wrangled the covers out from underneath her. She repositioned until she was lying down flat and he could pull the covers up around her before returning to the chair. He needed to send out a dozen emails explaining the situation.

The work only took half an hour. Tiredness was starting to kick in as he finished up the last message. Before turning off his laptop, he checked the vet camera. Loki was sleeping in a kennel, looking happy as a lark. Tiernan could get a few hours of shut-eye now, knowing Loki was fine and would be coming home tomorrow.

For a split second, he debated his next actions. Melody had been clear that she didn't want to be alone. He wasn't sure she intended to sleep in the same bed. Since he couldn't ask her, he took the chair instead, cutting the lights down on the dimmer switch. His room could be pitch-black if he turned everything off, which could scare Melody when she woke up. He could sleep under pretty much any conditions after growing up on a ranch during calving season.

Leaning back, chin to chest, he nodded off inside of two minutes.

"Hey." A familiar voice, Melody's voice, stirred him from sleep.

He blinked a couple of times to find Melody standing next to the chair. Her hand rested on his before tugging at him to stand up. He did, bringing his other hand up to wipe the sleep from his eyes.

"Don't wake up," she said before adding, "Come to bed with me where you'll be more comfortable."

Tiernan wasn't one to argue with a beautiful and intelligent woman asking him to go to bed. Besides, he could barely think through the tired fog. So, he did exactly as she asked, throwing the sheets and comforter up and climbing into bed after her. Certain body parts woke up when she curled her lean arms and legs around him.

She smelled like the air after a spring rain. Breathing in her scent wasn't helping him fall back asleep. It didn't take long for her steady, even breathing to indicate she'd drifted off. He didn't dare move since she didn't get much in the way of sleep last night. Her hair tickled his chest as she shifted, burrowing deeper into the crook of his arm.

This was as close to heaven as Tiernan figured he'd ever get.

It took another half hour but he finally found sleep again. Morning showed too quickly. The next time he opened his eyes it was half past six. Melody had rolled onto her other side, taking him with her. His leg was over one of hers and the sheets were in a tangle around them. If he stayed here much longer, he would never get out of bed.

Reluctantly, he untangled their arms and legs and then slipped out of the covers. He rubbed his eyes again before checking his laptop. The responses were starting to roll in and, thankfully, most everyone understood and wished him well. Said they'd be waiting for the saddles however long it took, and they would wrap the rendering of the saddles he'd provided instead. He truly had the best customers in Texas.

One of his emails came from his baby sister, Reese. Apparently, there was a storm brewing back home in Cider Creek. She didn't want to go home any more than he did based on her message, which essentially asked him to help her get out of it. He fired off a response, telling her that he would be home as soon as possible, and she needed to make up her own mind about returning. There was no way he was leaving Melody to deal with the sheriff alone.

His next move was to check on Loki. The dog was still sleeping, curled up with a stuffed sloth in his paws. It was darned near the most heartwarming scene he'd ever laid eyes on. As much as he missed his dog, it was probably for the best he was at the vet's and not running around with Tiernan and Melody, like they planned to do as soon as she was awake.

Tiernan stood up and stretched. Melody rolled over and blinked her eyes open.

"Hey," she said in a raspy, sleepy voice that tugged at what was left of his heartstrings.

"Good morning," he said, moving to the side of the bed where he sat down. "How did you sleep?"

"Better than I have in a long time," she admitted, then her cheeks turned three shades of red. "Comfortable bed."

He nodded and smirked. Comfortable bed his backside. With her, he'd slept deeper than he wanted to admit, too. They were at a standstill when it came to admitting the reason, which was fine with him. He'd faced down stubborn bulls before on the circuit. He could dig his heels in just as much.

"Have you heard from the vet about Loki?" she asked, pushing up to sitting. The blanket fell down to her full hips. She had just enough curves to be sexy, and they'd been imprinted on his body in the short time they were together last night. In fact, getting out of bed this morning had been difficult.

"There's a camera if you'd like to see him for yourself," he said, motioning toward the laptop.

"I'd like that a lot, actually," she said. "I had a dream that he was running around, causing trouble."

"He will be soon enough," Tiernan said on a chuckle. Her dream warmed his heart a couple more degrees. It was on low burn with her right now, and a spark was all it would take to start a raging wildfire inside him. He pulled up the vet's camera and pointed to Loki's kennel.

"Aww," she said. "Is he seriously hugging a stuffed animal?"

"Yes, he is," Tiernan confirmed.

"That is the sweetest thing I'll probably ever see," she said as she tilted her head to one side and clasped her hands together.

"How about your clients?" she asked as she situated a pillow behind her to lean back against. He didn't want to think about the thin cotton material of her shirt being the only barrier between his hands and her creamy skin. Or the fact she was in his bed and that made him feel like she belonged to him on a primal level.

"So far, so good," he said. "They've been understanding of the situation. At least the ones I've heard from so far."

"I'm sure the rest will be, too," she said. "The fire wasn't exactly your fault."

"Not yours, either," he quickly added before she could get too inside her head and blame herself again. He studied her for a long moment and decided she already had. "Do you always do that?"

"What?"

"Take responsibility for the world?" he asked in all sincerity. "There are a whole lot of things none of us have control over and never will." Growing up on a ranch dealing with livestock, weather conditions and Mother Nature had taught him the lesson well. Half the time, they were going on a wing and a prayer, hoping for the best.

She threw off the covers and climbed out of bed. "Speaking of which, we should get dressed and go see Coop before the vet calls to pick up Loki."

A serious wall had just come up between them. He took note of the fact she didn't want to hear his advice. Wasn't ready to accept it? From the looks of it, he'd struck a nerve.

MELODY HEADED FOR the bathroom. She realized midway that her stuff was in the guest bath, so she rerouted. Halfway there, she heard Tiernan rummaging around in the kitchen behind her as she crossed the room.

She splashed water on her face after brushing her teeth in the guest suite, then changed her clothing. A pair of jeans and a light green sweater would keep the chill off now that the temperature was dipping. Having so little material between her and Tiernan last night hadn't been the best of ideas. She'd neglected to tell him the dream she'd had about him. Suffice it to say, she woke up knowing full well if the two of them had sex the fireworks would light the sky from Texas to Tokyo.

The man had hit the nail on the head about her taking responsibility for the world, but she wasn't ready to hear those words from him or anyone else. She'd been doing just fine without someone poking around in her thoughts, no matter how devastatingly handsome the guy might be. His ability to read her was a little unsettling, too.

Besides, she needed to speak to her brother. She needed to look into Coop's eyes and ask about the note telling her to drive away from Austin. She needed to study his features when she asked if he knew anything about their half-brother. And she needed to see for herself if the muscle underneath his left eye twitched when she asked him about the break-in at their mother's place.

What lengths would Coop go to in order to protect their father? Would he be willing to throw his own sister under the bus? They hadn't been close in years. Granted, they didn't exactly call to check on each other or spend holidays together since she'd dumped her inheritance. Plus, she normally worked, which had been a great excuse to check out of a normal life. Burying herself in her job was one way to keep everyone at arm's length—a job she no longer had to worry about since she was out. The thought of doing nothing for a month or two until she figured out her next step would have scared old Melody. Staring down the possibility of prison time showed her there were far bigger problems to be faced than unemployment. Since she rarely ever went out or spent money on big ticket items, she had a decent amount in savings. Not enough to live off of for years, but she could get through a few months with her emergency fund if she was careful. There were family heirlooms that she'd been hanging on to. She could sell those if times got tight.

If her brother was willing to kill to protect the Cantor name, would he even consider how damning the evidence might be that was stacking against her? Or did he assume she wouldn't even be considered a slight possibility as a suspect? Would that have been the reason for the note being placed on her car? To cast suspicion somewhere else? Protect her from arrest?

Tiernan made good points early on in the investigation when he brought up the size issue, as well. She wouldn't be strong enough to lift an eighteen-year-old male, let alone carry him away from a vehicle with no signs of the body being dragged across the dirt and scrub.

The sheriff was locked on to her, though. Did he have other evidence? He wouldn't have to disclose everything to her attorney. Surely, he had something in his back pocket that he was hiding to keep circling him back to her. Did he believe Tiernan was in on it, too? The two of them were somehow in league with each other? Wouldn't it be easy enough to prove they'd never met before he'd volunteered to take the back seat of the deputy's SUV?

It was an angle the law might be looking into now that she really thought about it. Why would they be willing to be seen together now, though? Wouldn't that go against a secret affair? Or a business arrangement? The sheriff hadn't been too keen on Tiernan stepping in to help her when they were in his office. Was he trying to make a case against the both of them? She wished she could be a fly on the wall of his office to see what he was up to.

Heading back to the kitchen, she switched gears to caffeine and breakfast. She'd slept better last night than she could remember, but she wasn't ready to concede it was because Tiernan was in bed with her. His bed was far more comfortable than the couch she'd volunteered to sleep on the night before.

The smell of dark roast was enough to wake her up as she walked into the room. Seeing Tiernan standing in the kitchen, a lean hip against the counter, sent her heart racing, making the caffeine boost a little less necessary. Her throat suddenly dried up as she walked toward him. He held up a second mug.

"Thank you," she said. Clearing her throat

didn't help as much as she wanted it to. Taking a sip after blowing on the top of the coffee was better.

He mumbled something she couldn't quite scan and probably didn't need to hear. His presence in the room already had her body keenly aware of him. The fact he wasn't wearing a shirt didn't help matters much in the attraction department.

"We can grab breakfast on the road if you want to get going soon," she said.

He answered with a slight nod. The man's carved-from-granite face and intense eyes made for one helluva package. The word *perfection* came to mind, even though he'd laugh at the description. "Might as well head out since the vet wants to keep Loki a few more hours." He started toward the bedroom. "I'll throw on a shirt."

Melody had no comment even though a few protests came to mind. She finished her coffee and put on her shoes. She still hadn't checked all her phone messages but had made a dent. Fifty-seven texts. Melody had forgotten how bad it was with all that had happened since she'd last checked her phone.

The threatening email came back to mind. Would the sheriff explain that away as her trying to make herself seem innocent? Would he suspect either her or Tiernan of doing that to throw off suspicion?

The man needed to have his head checked out because there were some serious deficiencies in his logic. She tucked her cell inside her purse and walked over to the door.

Tiernan returned, looking better than any man had a right to in a black long-sleeve cotton shirt that fit him to a tee. He finished off his coffee before setting the mug inside the sink and heading toward her.

She checked the time. "We should get to my brother's before he leaves for work. It'll probably be best to surprise him at home anyway."

Tiernan nodded. He started to say something but stopped himself. What was that about?

"He has a few 'tells,' so I should be able to read him better in person than on the phone," she said in more of a defensive tone than intended. She shook her head as though she could somehow shake off the giveaway that she was nervous about the visit.

Tiernan held the door open for her but he held his tongue. He also didn't comment on her statement, which spoke volumes.

Could she get answers from Coop? Did she really want to know if her brother was capable of murder? Because she had an ominous feeling she was about to find out.

Chapter Seventeen

The ride to Melody's brother's house north of Austin was quiet. The quick stop for fast-food breakfast sandwiches and coffee refills was the only interruption in the hour-and-a-half drive. The houses in this subdivision were new and looked like mini mansions. They also all looked alike with their brick facades and castle-like features.

"His SUV is parked out front," Melody said. It was a top-of-the-line Lincoln Navigator in shiny gold. There was a red Porsche beside it. The house and the vehicles said flashy money, a stark contrast to Melody, who drove a small sedan and wore jeans. They hugged every single curve to perfection, but she wasn't exactly dripping in jewels. Nor did she care, which was an even bigger point. "And his secondary car is here, too."

Melody and her brother couldn't be more opposite on the surface.

"What about a wife and kids?" he asked as he circled the block.

"He's married but no children yet," she said. "I think they were trying before our father's arrest and then put it on hold."

"Will his wife be home?" he asked.

"She travels a lot for work, so my guess is no," she said. "When she is home, I think she parks inside the garage."

"Who corroborated your brother's alibi?" Tiernan asked.

"I'd have to ask the lawyer or the sheriff," she said. "The law must have been by to interview my brother by now, along with my mother."

"Did she mention a visit?" he asked.

"As a matter of fact, all she talked about was the break-in and how much stress she was under because of it and the stuff going on with my father," she responded. "She expressed concern for Coop and the way the case was affecting her reputation."

His grip tightened on the steering wheel at the reminder. He'd heard Melody's side of the conversation and had wanted to shake her mother. The woman had an amazing daughter but only seemed concerned about her son. He was proud of Melody for calling her mother out on it even though it didn't seem to come easy for her.

"I'm sorry," he said.

She reached over and touched his forearm as he parked at the house across the street from her brother's. "You didn't do anything wrong."

"Doesn't mean I'm not sorry someone else didn't treat you the way you deserve to be treated," he said with sincerity. "Your mother is lucky to have a daughter as kind and considerate as you are. Not to mention the fact you already hold the world on your shoulders. What does your brother do that's so special?"

"He's Coop," she said with a shrug. "He's always been the golden boy of the family."

"Idiots," Tiernan said before adding, "I shouldn't insult your parents like that, but hell…"

"Believe me, you're not hurting my feelings," she said. "My only ties come out of a sense of obligation." She issued a sharp sigh. "Honestly, they were a lot nicer to me before I ditched my trust fund. I think that was the ultimate slap in the face. Like I wasn't part of them any longer. I didn't blindly accept my father's behavior, and money wasn't the be-all and end-all in my life. I highly doubt they understand me."

Tiernan leaned across the divider and pressed a kiss to her lips. "You're a very special person and you should know it."

The red blush that crawled up her neck and settled on her cheeks was sexier than lacy lingerie. Not that he would mind that, either. When she showed her emotions—which he'd noticed was rare—her vulnerability made her darn near irresistible.

"I have a feeling arguing with you would be the equivalent of trying to negotiate with a bull," she said with a smile. "So, I won't even try. I will say thank you, though, and leave it at that."

"Fair enough."

Tiernan exited his side of the truck and rounded the front to open her door for her. She took the hand he offered and kept hold as they made their way toward the house after closing the door. He took a detour to touch the hood of the Lincoln. It was warm. By the time they reached the oversize wooden front door, she had a death grip. Before moving any farther, he stopped her at a point where the Navigator would block them from view.

He rounded on her and brought his free hand up to run his thumb along her jawline. The pull toward kissing her was the force of a tornado moments after touchdown. When his thumb grazed her bottom lip, the urge doubled down.

"I can take the lead with him if you're not feeling it," he said to her, locking on to those incredible golden-brown eyes.

For a minute, the world shrank to the two of them. She slicked her tongue across her lip, leaving a silky trail, and nearly obliterating his will-power in the process.

"He's my brother," she said. "I can handle him." She paused for a few beats. "I'm just afraid of what I'm about to see in his eyes."

She didn't say the word *murderer*, but he knew exactly what she meant.

Tiernan tilted his chin toward the house. "I hope you get the answers you want."

"So do I," she said, then took in a deep breath like people did when they were about to jump off a cliff. "Let's do this."

He stepped aside to let her lead the way. She immediately reached back for his hand and then linked their fingers. Ready or not, they were about to face her brother.

MELODY RANG THE doorbell and waited. She had half a mind to call her brother to make certain he answered, figuring no one actually came to the door anymore. Except Coop did after another round of church bell sounds.

"Hey," he said, his gaze bouncing from her to Tiernan and back. "Everything okay?"

The top two buttons of her brother's crisp white shirt were unbuttoned. His tie was loose around his neck.

She tightened her grip on Tiernan's hand. "I

just wanted to stop by and ask a few questions. This is my friend Tiernan."

"Nice to meet you," Coop said, after sizing up her companion. Her brother wasn't exactly being subtle. The way his face muscles tensed gave away his disdain for her companion.

Tiernan, on the other hand, offered a polite smile and a handshake.

"Can we come inside?" she asked.

Coop's gaze skimmed the area like he half expected law enforcement to jump out of the bushes. She could think of plenty of reasons her brother might be jumpy and none of them had to do with being overcaffeinated.

"Sure," Coop conceded after checking his Rolex. "I have a couple of minutes before I need to head out for work."

"We won't be long," Melody said. "We have an important package to pick up soon."

Tiernan followed her inside the entryway of her brother's palatial home. Coop had darker hair. His muddy-brown eyes were cradled by dark circles. As much as Melody didn't want to read too much into her brother's nervous disposition, it was hard not to under the circumstances. Melody reminded herself that Coop had been stepping in at work to take their father's place while the business was under investigation, and also while maintaining the man's innocence in corporate affairs.

Coop took exactly five steps into the two-story foyer, stopped and then spun around on them. "What can I help you with today?" Up close, his complexion was ruddy and stress cracks were permanently etched around his eyes and mouth. All signs of the carefree, life-comes-easy brother from years ago were gone. The one who made the family proud on the sports field, oftentimes being carried on his teammates' shoulders after a game-winning play, was no longer the person standing in front of her. Instead, she stared into bloodshot mud orbs.

"Did you hear about the break-in at Mom's?" she asked, tilting her head to one side as she examined Coop.

He threw his hands in the air. "I'm just glad she wasn't home at the time. Who knows what might have happened then."

"Interesting to note not much was taken," she continued with a nod of acknowledgment. "And, yes, I'm relieved our mother is fine."

"I'm guessing the person was casing the place," Coop said a little too enthusiastically. Besides, when did he use terms like "casing" during normal conversation? Was he watching cop shows all of a sudden?

"Could have been," Melody said. "I'm sure

the law will conduct a thorough investigation and nail the bastard responsible."

She caught a two-second flash of emotion pass behind his eyes. Again, she was scrutinizing her brother and it might not be warranted. Everyone in the family had been through a lot since their father's arrest. Coop had taken it the hardest since he worked most closely with their dad.

"Yes," he said. "That's the hope."

"Do you think we should hire our own investigators?" she asked, reaching for something to catch him off guard with. "Just in case the police aren't as thorough as we would like them to be?"

"It's an idea," Coop said, his voice unchanged. "We can talk it over." He folded his arms. "It might be spending money unnecessarily, though. With Dad's legal troubles, money isn't as free-flowing as it used to be."

"The expenses must be racking up," Melody said. "I'd help if I could."

"Your inheritance is gone," Coop said quickly. A little too quickly? She must have shot a look because he added, "You gave it away a long time ago and divorced yourself from the family financially. No one expects you to pick up now and suddenly start contributing."

"Speaking of family," Melody said. "Where's Janice?"

"Dubai," he said. "She's been there all month with her charity league."

Melody nodded before redirecting the subject. "Have the police been here lately?"

Coop's eyes widened to saucers, and he didn't blink. "No. Why?"

"Just curious," she said. "With the theft at Mom's place, I thought maybe they'd stopped by to question you."

"I was the first one Mom called when this happened," Coop said. "They talked to me at Mom's place since I went over immediately."

"Oh, really," she said. His normal "tell" signs conflicted with each other. "I only just found out about it."

"I told Mom not to call and worry you," he said.

"Why would you do that?" she questioned. What reason on earth could he have for wanting to keep something as important as their mother's home being broken into from her?

"Because you have enough on your plate with the job search," he said.

Since when did her brother start keeping such close tabs on her? Melody wanted to believe this was all out of good will, but her gut instincts were picking up on red flags. Coop was hiding something.

"Where were you that night when Mom called?" she asked.

"I was at a Longhorn game and stayed at the family cabin," he said. She must have shot quite the look because he immediately said, "Do you want to see the receipts?"

Given he was so quick to offer, she declined. Coop loved his alma mater and was involved as an alumnus.

Before she became too defensive about their mother not making any secret out of favoring Coop over Melody, she said, "I'm glad you were there for her. She didn't quite sound herself on the phone."

"The whole event shook her up," he said.

"I can only imagine how awful and violated she must have felt to have her personal space invaded like that," Melody said, thinking about the parallel to Tiernan's workshop—a workshop he'd obviously lovingly built and took great pride in. Frustration settled over her along with a weighty feeling of helplessness that had no business on her shoulders.

"I'm just glad I wasn't too far. I got to her pretty fast," he said by way of explanation.

Melody's mom had remarried and then divorced. Although she enjoyed living alone, her mother had never acquired a taste for solitary life. Melody wouldn't be surprised if the woman wasn't already scouting her next husband despite the divorce being less than a year old.

"You guys don't have to protect me from everything," Melody said. "I would have liked to have known sooner."

"You're my little sis," Coop said, pulling emotional strings that took her back to their childhood. "I'm always going to look out for a Cantor."

The warm and fuzzy feeling Melody had experienced faded when her brother added the last bit. Because the look in his eyes said he was dead serious.

"Could I ask a question, if it's not too much trouble?" Tiernan interrupted. He squeezed her hand slightly. She took the gesture to mean she should trust him.

Coop didn't look thrilled. Then again, her brother hadn't been real excited to see either one of them since he opened the front door to find them standing there. "Depends on what it is."

Her brother's response caught her off guard. He'd been in defensive mode the whole conversation. The visit she'd hoped would answer some of her questions, and hopefully clear her brother, had backfired.

"I'll take that to mean I can go forward," Tiernan said. "Have you been home all morning?"

Chapter Eighteen

"Yes. I'm about to leave, though," Coop said. Tiernan knew he was lying.

"We don't want to hold you up," Tiernan said, tugging at Melody's hand. They'd gotten all they were going to from her brother. There would be no confessions coming from this guy. He was too busy covering his tracks. His attitude was as prickly as a startled porcupine. He was guilty as sin for something, but Tiernan didn't want to condemn the man without proof.

Melody followed Tiernan's lead, walking outside beside him.

"Take care of yourself, Coop," she said to her brother. "You look tired, like you haven't slept in days."

"I'll be fine," Coop said. The man was a brick wall when it came to having any tender feelings toward his family. Despite their differences, Tiernan never once doubted any one of his family members would have his back with one phone call. It shouldn't be a rare quality among siblings, but he was beginning to realize just how much it was. He was also starting to think he needed to head home, if only to reconnect with his brothers and sisters. Looking back now, he was embarrassed at how much he'd neglected his relationship with his mother and grandmother. Duncan Hayes should never have been granted that power—power they'd all handed over to the man who'd seemed larger than life when they were kids.

"I mean it," Melody said to her brother. She let go of Tiernan's hand before walking toward Coop and hugging him. "Let me know if you need help with anything."

"Have you been to see Dad?" Coop asked after the brief hug that he'd returned more out of a sense of obligation than anything else, based on the man's expression.

"No," she admitted. "We've talked on the phone, though. He told me not to come."

"Probably doesn't want his children to see him locked behind bars like some kind of animal," Coop said with disdain.

"People have to suffer the consequences of their actions, Coop," Melody said with compassion.

Her brother bristled. "Only when they do something wrong. Our father is innocent." The insistence with which he spoke those words came across more like trying to wish something into reality as opposed to believing it to be true. It reeked of desperation that caused Tiernan to have doubts. Some folks believed if they said something over and over again, it would eventually become the truth. That sounded like the case here.

"I know you want to believe that, Coop," Melody said. "So do I. But the evidence says otherwise." She stared at her brother for a long moment. "Do you have a good attorney?"

"The same one Dad has, but I won't need him," Coop said with more defensiveness in his tone.

"You should get a lawyer separate from the company and definitely different than Dad's," she said. "I'm no expert on the law, but it seems like a good idea to have someone who can differentiate your case from our dad's."

Coop's gaze narrowed and his lips thinned. His sister was looking out for him but his response to her was to be angry. Granted, the man didn't appear to want to hear anything that might be considered contrary to his own opinion. Tiernan had stared down bulls with less of a stubborn streak. Coop had decided he was right and had no plans to alter his opinions despite a mountain of evidence pointing toward his father's guilt.

"I'm fine," Coop said with impatience. He was like a teapot just shy of boiling over.

"Of course you are," Melody soothed. She was trying to bring a sense of calm to a situation that had gone south from the minute Coop laid eyes on them.

"I've already thought through it all," Coop continued. He might be listening, but the man wasn't truly hearing a word coming out of Melody's mouth. His brain was already clicking ahead to whatever defense he might need to mount next. "Hey, sis, I appreciate your concern."

The about-face caught Melody off guard, based on her expression and lack of an immediate response. Coop was good at manipulation. Was he capable of murder?

Sizing him up, Coop was sturdy enough to carry an eighteen-year-old. Melody mentioned something about her brother having been a college athlete, so there was that. He appeared to keep up some kind of workout, based on his general muscle tone. He was decently tall—over six feet tall. He'd proven willing to go to great lengths to protect the family name. His loyalty to their father didn't come across as sincere. It was more like self-preservation. Prescott would have investigators dig into the Cantor family business records to make sure Coop didn't have any involvement in the crimes. Based on Tiernan's understanding, the family had their hands in a few pies. Some of the revenue was from legitimate sources. The illegal income came from their father. *Alleged* illegal income.

"Be careful, Coop," Melody said, not budging from in front of her brother. "I don't just mean legally."

"I'm fine," came the response.

"One more question before we go," Melody said before taking a step back and reaching for Tiernan's hand. He had a premonition that she was about to drop a bomb.

"Shoot," Coop said.

"What do you know about Jason Riker?" she asked.

Coop's mouth fell open before it snapped shut. "Pretty much everything everyone else knows. A kid was murdered in a nearby county and there aren't obvious signs as to the reason."

"Really?" Melody's disappointment in her brother was apparent by the expression on her face and tone in her voice.

"What?" Coop asked, trying to play innocent when he clearly knew more. "Should I know more about him?"

"Other than the fact he's our half-brother?" Melody asked.

"No way," Coop said. "The only people who belong in our family have the last name Cantor."

"It wasn't his fault that he didn't," she countered, much to Coop's disgust. And *disgust* was the only word to describe the look on his face.

"How could you betray us and claim this kid as a relative?" Coop asked.

"Are you kidding me right now?" she asked, fist on her left hip. Tiernan squeezed her right hand. It was time to go. The conversation was getting heated and that wouldn't go anywhere useful. They had the information they needed to move forward. Anything more than this was going to be pure frustration, like beating a dead horse. But Tiernan had no plans to interfere with family matters. He squeezed Melody's hand again in an attempt to ground her. A look passed behind her eyes that told him she understood.

Rather than debate her side, Melody held a hand up to stop her brother from responding. "Look, I didn't mean to offend you. I agree that the Cantor name is special and worth protecting. Our dad shouldn't be in jail if he's innocent. You'll get one hundred percent agreement with me on that point. And, Coop, I truly hope that he is innocent. I can scarcely think about another outcome. I *want* everything to work out the same as you do. So, I'll leave it at that."

Coop nodded. The man was going to great lengths to protect his family's legacy. Was Duncan Hayes any different? Probably not. And it was the main reason Tiernan was unable to respect Coop. He'd experienced firsthand a person who cared more about image than substance. Tiernan would take a hard pass on believing in someone like them. He and Melody got what they came for. Now he needed to get her out of there.

THERE WERE SO many thoughts running through Melody's head right now it was like a pinball machine on full tilt. The only tether to reality was Tiernan. The way he squeezed her hand said it was time to go. She listened. They walked away. *Disappointment* wasn't nearly a big enough word to describe how she felt about her brother right now. Why was she so surprised, though? Coop acted exactly as she'd feared he would. Sketchy.

The way he'd initially pretended not to know who Jason was sickened her.

Melody walked away with Tiernan after a quick goodbye to Coop. Disappointment sat heavy on her chest because she also realized her brother was hiding something.

Once she was settled inside the truck, she

stared over at her brother. He was hastily moving to his SUV while having a conversation on his cell phone. She had no doubt he was covering his tracks.

"What do you think of Coop?" she asked Tiernan as he drove away. Her brother's house quickly filled the rearview.

"Probably the same as you," Tiernan said honestly. She appreciated him for it.

"He's guilty as sin," she said, hating that she had to say those words about her own brother. Facing things head-on had been an acquired taste for her, having grown up in a family famous for sweeping everything under the rug, including her father's infidelity.

"I know," Tiernan confirmed. "He lied about not being gone this morning. His Lincoln was hot to the touch. There's only one reason for that."

Melody gasped. "He was driving it before we even got there."

"That's right," Tiernan confirmed with a frown. He clearly didn't enjoy bringing her bad news about her family member. In fact, based on his expression, he didn't think it was his place at all. Except that he must realize she deserved to know what was going on and that her brother was trying to pull the wool over her eyes.

"I had a bad feeling the whole time we were

talking that he was lying to me or hiding something. I couldn't quite put my finger on it," she confirmed. "You're right to tell me your observations, by the way."

"It's not what I wanted to see, if that makes a difference," he said.

"Actually, it does," she said. "I've never been all that close to Coop. He's always been the older brother who was more into his friends than staying at home on a weekend night to be with me. However, I did idolize him for a long time and I felt that instinct kicking in."

"He made no secret about trying to play that card with you," he continued. "For instance, the whole 'little sis' bit was contrived." He glanced over at her as he navigated onto the highway. "I'm sorry."

"No. Don't be," she argued. "I need to hear it because I'm always going to have a soft spot for my brother. We grew up together. He's my family."

"Funny how family can manipulate us," he said with the kind of wistfulness that said there was a story behind those words. Since she needed a distraction from her own family drama, she decided to ask about Tiernan's.

"What happened in yours, if you don't mind my asking?"

"My father died when I was in elementary

school," he started. "My grandfather stepped in to be 'the man' of the family and destroyed it instead."

"I'm sorry to hear that, Tiernan," she said. "Is that why you don't live on your family's ranch?"

"It's a big part of it," he said. "We all jumped ship the minute we turned eighteen."

"What about your mother? Are the two of you close?" she asked.

"Looking back now, I was a jerk to take off the way I did," he said. "She did her best to mediate. I think she just wanted us to have something from our dad and that was the reason she put up with her father-in-law."

"You were barely out of high school when you left," she said. "We all thought we had life figured out back then, didn't we?"

He chuckled, and it was the first break in tension this morning. "I can't speak for you but I was an arrogant little twit. More testosterone than common sense."

"I read somewhere our brains aren't fully developed until we're twenty, so there's that," she said.

"Explains a lot of my bad choices early in life," he said. "Not the ones I made later, I'm afraid."

Tiernan was finally opening up about his personal life, so she decided to capitalize on the moment.

"A story like that always begins with a romance," she said, ignoring the flush she felt along with the twinge of jealousy.

"I recently made a bad decision there, too," he said. "Guess I can't blame youth, hormones and inexperience on that one."

"People can slip past the radar," she said. "Doesn't mean we're stupid. Just means we actually trusted someone who took advantage of us."

His self-deprecating laugh probably shouldn't charm her. "When you put it like that, I don't feel like as much of an idiot."

"You're not," she said. "Believe me. We've all been there at one time or another."

"Explain," he urged.

"I was engaged after college," she admitted. Before he could accuse her of baiting him to get his secrets, she added, "Looking back, he would have turned out just like my father and brother. We were the 'perfect' couple on the outside. Both came from politically climbing families. My father approved very much, despite the fact Brently Fox would have cheated behind my back and never truly loved me. Between that and my father's behavior in general, I stopped trusting everyone a very long time ago."

Tiernan studied the stretch of road in front

of him for a long moment. "Sounds like a lonesome way to live."

"When you put it like that, it is," she conceded. "I never get hurt, though." To say she had daddy issues was a lot like saying brown was a color. But she was just beginning to realize how deep those scars were.

"Never take a risk. Never get burned," he agreed, nodding. Then his tone changed. "I rode broncos when I was younger and there were rides that scared the hell out of me deep down. I never let those fears take the wheel. Fear is good. It's built in us to keep us alive. Sure doesn't make us happy, though. Some of the highlights of my career came because I stared those fears in the eyes and dared them to do their best."

"I can't imagine how scary your job must have been," she said, not quite ready to run toward the unknown or what scared her. "I've always taken a safe route there, too." Looking over her life so far, she'd never pushed out of her comfort zone until recently. And despite the dangerous circumstances, she'd never felt more alive.

Could she face down her fear enough to ask Tiernan what she wanted? One night of distraction. One night of getting lost with him. One night of what would be the best sex of her life?

She opened her mouth to speak, then clamped it shut when his cell started buzzing.

Chapter Nineteen

"Where the hell are you?" Prescott asked. He'd never been one to lose his composure, so Tiernan was taken aback. This wasn't a good sign considering they were in the middle of a murder investigation and the sheriff had blinders on when it came to other suspects.

"Anywhere you want us to be," he responded, hoping this new development wasn't as bad as he feared it might be. "Why?"

"How fast can you get home?" Prescott continued.

"Half an hour," he responded. He'd have to push the speed limit. "Do we get to know why?"

"I'll tell you when you get there," Prescott said before ending the call.

"I should probably call Bebe and let her know we can't come tonight for dinner," she said. "I hated having to cancel last night, especially since she sounded so disappointed."

A half dozen thoughts slammed into Tiernan's

mind. None he liked. "Go ahead and do that. In the meantime, I'll see about how fast I can get us back to my place."

Melody dug in her purse for her cell, producing it a few seconds later. She made the call and waited. "Rolled into voice mail." She paused for a few seconds. "She might be at work right now, so hopefully she'll reach out."

He nodded. His thoughts bounced from the interaction with Coop to what on earth could be waiting for them back at his place. His next thought was Loki. He hated the thought of leaving him at the vet any longer than necessary. It didn't seem like they had enough time to swing by and pick him up.

"You're worried, aren't you?" Melody asked. "You get these deep grooves in your forehead that give you away."

"Remind me never to play poker with you," he conceded. "I guess I never noticed since I rarely check the mirror."

"How bad is it?" she asked. "In your mind, at least."

"I have half a mind not to show," he admitted.

"But?"

"That would be like admitting guilt to whatever we're about to be accused of," he said.

"You don't think good evidence might have

surfaced that we need to be told about in person?" she continued.

"We'll know soon enough." He didn't intend for those words to come out like the world was ending. Hearing how they sounded, he needed to clarify. "At least Prescott is asking us to come home. I'm thinking in a worst-case scenario, he would tell me to drive to the sheriff's office where he would meet us."

A sigh of relief filled the space between them.

"I didn't mean to worry you," he clarified. She must've assumed the sheriff could come to arrest her any minute with the way the case had been moving so far.

"It's not your fault," she said. It was, in a sense, because he could have been choosing his words more carefully. "I've never been in this position before and the sheriff seems locked on to figuring out how I'm responsible. I'm still scratching my head as to why. If anyone in my family was guilty, it would have to be my brother."

"His alibi checks out," Tiernan said. "He said he had receipts if you're talking about the break-in at your mother's place."

"I'm not surprised he would be at a Longhorn sporting event," she said. "It's the trip I'm more concerned about. How do we know he went anywhere?"

"There wouldn't be hotel receipts," he said, thinking out loud.

"That's right—he has a cabin, so there's not really a good way to track him there," she said. "Actually, it belongs to the family. I just never go since I cut myself off financially. Plus, how could I enjoy staying anywhere that was potentially bought with other people's retirement income that had been stolen from them?"

"Do you still have a key to the place?" he asked. A quick trip out there might answer a few questions about her brother's alibi.

"Yes," she said. "I've been too lazy to return it."

Somehow, he doubted she'd be too lazy to do anything. He would believe her more if she blamed the slip on an overly busy schedule. She'd already admitted to working all the time to the point of sacrificing a social life. Then again, since Corinne, he could be accused of doing the same. "It might be time to visit the family cabin."

"After we face the music with Prescott," she said. The visit must've been weighing heavily on her mind, considering the fact she'd been tapping her index finger on the door handle for several minutes now. The tempo picked up with her stress levels. He had a tell when he was concerned and so did she.

Since they were almost there at this point, he didn't answer. They could swing by the house and find out what bomb her lawyer was about to drop. Next, they could drop by the vet's office for Loki. After, they could head toward her family cabin to poke around and see what they could find. On their way back, they could take time to visit with Bebe. It was a full schedule. Since he didn't have any work to do, he could spare the time. Besides, something was niggling at the back of his mind since the visit with Coop, and he couldn't quite put his finger on it.

Tiernan pulled onto his gravel drive and headed down the lane leading to his cabin. Back at Hayes Cattle Ranch, there was security twenty-four seven. This place was home and, until yesterday, wasn't in need of protecting like a livestock business worth millions of dollars. His small business was successful by most standards. It brought in enough for him to live comfortably and never have to touch his inheritance. He, like Melody, didn't care about the money in the way most folks did. As long as he had a decent roof over his head and plenty of food on the table, he considered himself well-off. His banker would classify him as a millionaire, but a million dollars didn't go as far these days. Now, the big deals were billionaires. Tiernan had no interest in reaching that stratosphere of wealth. He did just fine on what he made.

Prescott's SUV was parked in front of the cabin. The lawyer's arms were crossed as he leaned against his vehicle. He must have been standing there for quite some time.

Pulling up alongside him, Tiernan parked and exited the truck. He made an immediate cut around the front end of his vehicle in order to open Melody's door for her. Prescott followed. As soon as she exited the passenger side, he started with the news.

"The sheriff was on his way to bring Melody in for questioning," Prescott started, his tone heated. "I told him that I'd do the honors and that, as her attorney, I had a right to speak to her first anyway. I don't, by the way. But the sheriff didn't seem ready to push my buttons."

"Why would he want me to come in all of a sudden?" Melody asked, confusion drawing her eyebrows together. "All we did was sleep last night."

"Where have you been?" Prescott whirled around on them mid-pace.

"Out for breakfast," Tiernan cut in, not wanting Melody to have to answer. It was a partial truth. They technically had eaten food on the way down to Austin.

Prescott threw his hands up in the air. "I can't

help you unless you trust me one hundred percent with the truth."

Melody shot a glance at Tiernan. One he recognized as her wanting to come clean. So, he gave a slight nod.

"I asked Tiernan if we could visit my brother this morning before we picked up Loki from the vet," she started.

Prescott looked ready to blow. "Why would you do that?" He paced the length of the truck. "Don't you trust me to handle this case? Because these day trips are hurting us more than you realize."

"What's that supposed to mean?" Tiernan asked, doing his level best to contain anger that was raging toward the surface.

Prescott stopped, dug his heels in the gravel and said, "Bebe Riker is dead and the last person on her cell phone records is Melody."

She gasped, immediately bringing her hand up to cover her mouth.

"We visited her and then you phoned her. We had plans," Tiernan said.

"I just called her again in the truck on the way over here," Melody admitted. "We were supposed to go over last night for dinner and—"

"I know," Prescott interrupted. "One of her employees overheard you making plans."

"How on earth? We were in the parking lot

when we had that conversation and there was no one else around," Melody quipped.

"This is a reminder you both need to hear. Someone is always around either watching or listening. You were the last one in contact with Bebe on her cell and you had plans. Any district attorney worth his or her salt would come after you for the murder, building more of a case against you," Prescott said, his voice toned down a few notches at this point. Tiernan couldn't fault the lawyer for being frustrated with them. They probably shouldn't have gone out on their own without consulting him or at least dropping a text after the fact. Those last words, though, resonated.

Tiernan sat on the information while Prescott continued.

"As your attorney, I need to know what moves you're making that might make my job even more difficult," he said.

Melody sat down right there on the gravel, cross-legged, a mix of emotions flashing behind her eyes. Anger. Sadness. Guilt. Regret. Tiernan had an overwhelming urge to give her a hand up and then bring her into an embrace.

"Give us a minute," he practically growled to the lawyer. From the corner of his eye, he saw Prescott's jaw nearly drop to the ground when he'd pulled Melody against his chest and then looped his arms around her waist.

Prescott disappeared inside his own vehicle a second later. He had questions about their relationship. The sheriff had insinuated they'd pulled this off as a couple. Being a couple would damage both of their defenses. So being a couple wasn't something Tiernan could afford to want. It wouldn't be good for Melody. *For Melody's case*, he corrected.

MELODY PULLED AWAY from Tiernan and forced her chin up. Two lives were lost…and for what? The senseless loss was staggering. The fire was clearly an attempt on her and Tiernan's lives. If they hadn't escaped, there would be four people dead. And to what end? Three of those people were tied together by one man… Henry Cooper Cantor II.

What about her brother, Coop? Why was he safe? Or was he? Was someone knocking down the Cantor children one at a time?

"I'm okay," she finally said to Tiernan. His face twisted and she immediately knew he could tell she was fudging the truth. "I'll *be* okay." She needed a minute to breathe and process what was happening so she could decide her next steps.

"Take your time," Tiernan said, ever the sea of calm. She had no idea what she would've done without him over the past couple of days. She'd grown to depend on his steady nature even though he caused butterflies to release in her chest. Trust wasn't something she was used to giving freely, so she was walking in foreign territory. He hadn't given her a reason not to believe he would be there as much as she needed him to be. Not only had he volunteered to help her see this through, but he was also following through on the commitment. Until he showed her otherwise, she would risk believing in him.

Melody took a couple of laps around the truck to work off some of her stress. She returned to speak to Tiernan, who gave a nod for Prescott to join them. The lawyer did and the three of them resumed their conversation.

"I suggested we go speak to my brother because I believe in my heart that I would be able to see right through him if he lied to me," she said by way of apology. "If you want to point a finger at someone, blame me."

"I'm trying to keep you out of prison," Prescott said in a far calmer voice now. "And I'm trying to keep others from accusing you of a crime you didn't commit."

She nodded and thanked him.

"Was he lying?" Prescott asked.

"Yes," she admitted. As much as she didn't want to deliver the news, it was the honest truth.

"His vehicle was warm, even though he denied leaving home this morning," Tiernan interjected. "He also said he could produce tickets to the Longhorn game he was at during the break-in and theft at their mother's home." He paused long enough to clench his back teeth. "Something you said a few minutes ago resonated with me. There's surveillance everywhere, so we should be able to track down whether or not he was actually at the game."

Prescott was nodding and taking notes on his cell phone.

"We felt bad for Jason's mother," Melody said. "It's the main reason we went to see her. My father rejected his own child. The kid was doing well until he tracked down his biological father. Then, he spiraled." She didn't speak the words that having any contact with her father was toxic. They hung in the air anyway. "We were planning to have dinner with her last night when the fire broke out and changed our plans."

"Speaking of cameras," Prescott started. "What about here?"

"I didn't lock my doors before this situation occurred," Tiernan admitted. "Why would I think I had a need for watching a deer cross my lawn?"

"Fair point. This area is considered one of the safest," Prescott agreed.

"Not much else beats it except for my hometown of Cider Creek," Tiernan added. She would like to go there someday. Possibly even meet his family. His mother had been through hell and back, but she must be a remarkable person if she brought up six children after losing the love of her life. The woman got brownie points for surviving a loss of that magnitude and being able to march ahead. It didn't sound like she'd remarried, either. Instead, she'd stayed on at a ranch to be near the man she loved. Tiernan hadn't said those exact words but it wasn't hard to put two and two together.

"The paper from the note on Melody's vehicle and the one in Jason's pocket matched," Prescott said, confirming they most likely came from the same source.

"My brother said he took a trip to our family cabin." Melody hopped back in the conversation. "Tiernan and I were planning to pick up Loki on our way to check it out. There would be signs if he'd visited recently."

Prescott nodded. "Would you be considered trespassing?"

"I know where the spare key is," she said a little too defensively.

"Be careful," Prescott instructed, not that he needed to. Melody had no plans to let her guard down.

"We will," Tiernan promised.

"Let me know whatever you find, if anything," Prescott further requested. "Take pictures and treat the place like a crime scene."

"Got it," Tiernan said. He'd talked about growing up on a cattle ranch. She intended to ask him why he was so good at investigations.

Prescott tucked his cell phone away. "I'll see what I can do about getting footage from the Longhorn game on the night of the break-in. I suspect a ticket was bought but never used. And I'll work it out with the sheriff so you don't have to go to his office. He can go through me for information for the time being."

"Speaking of which, information is a two-way street, right?" Tiernan asked the lawyer, who nodded. They exchanged quick goodbyes before Prescott headed out. The lawyer's vehicle kicked up dust from the gravel, causing it to disappear.

"Can we pick up Loki now?" Melody asked, waving her hand in the air, missing the black Lab who was a bundle of energy and unconditional love. He had convinced her that she needed a dog in her life.

"Let's go," Tiernan said, motioning toward the truck.

Loki was the easy part. It was a no-brainer to see him. The cabin? Not so much after what had happened during her last visit.

Chapter Twenty

Loki was a sight for sore eyes as Dr. Paul brought him out to the parking lot. Tiernan took a knee as the energetic Lab came bolting toward him. Impact nearly knocked Tiernan over so he put a hand down behind him for balance.

"He did great last night," Dr. Paul said as Melody dropped down next to Tiernan. He didn't hate having her by his side. Loki bounced from him to her and back in a heartbeat, taking all the affection he could get out of them.

It did the heart good to see him in such great shape.

"Everything checks out?" Tiernan asked.

"He's fit as a fiddle," Dr. Paul said. "Already had a hearty breakfast and a few extra treats for being such a good patient."

Loki ran over to the grassy area in the empty lot and took care of business. Tiernan stood and went through the motions of checking his empty pockets for a bag.

"Ralph will take care of that," Dr. Paul said. He and his partner had gone into business together years ago instead of having children.

"Thank you," Tiernan said. "And thank you for everything you did for Loki."

Dr. Paul's smile was ear to ear. The pride he took in his work showed in times like these. Melody surprised both of them by walking over and giving Dr. Paul a quick hug.

"This guy has become very important to all of us it seems," she said, motioning toward the black Lab that had bounded over to her side. If that didn't twist Tiernan's insides, he didn't know what would. Hearing her say those words stirred more of the feelings he'd been trying to avoid since Corinne. When he really thought about it, he'd never felt this kind of connection to his ex. Melody was the new bar for future relationships.

"Loki is special," Dr. Paul said before adding, "There are no follow-up instructions. He doesn't need any medication and can go on living his normal spoiled life."

"Will do," Tiernan said before walking over to his truck with Loki in tow. Tiernan opened the door and the Lab jumped right inside. Melody followed after taking the hand he'd offered, reclaiming the passenger seat. By the time she'd clicked on her seat belt, Tiernan had exchanged a handshake with Dr. Paul.

Sliding into the driver's seat, he was struck at how suddenly Melody had shown up in his world. But then life was full of surprises. He needed to take note of that fact the next time storm clouds covered the sun and his world darkened.

She gave him the address to the family cabin, which he immediately plugged into the GPS. They had a little more than an hour to kill. Longer if they stopped off for food.

Traffic wasn't bad. The burritos were even better. The cabin took ten extra minutes to reach after the stop at the largest gas station/convenience store in the state. They needed a Buc-ee's in Cider Creek. The promise of clean bathrooms along with more fuel pumps, food options, and road snacks than anyone could imagine made pit stops here a destination. Then again, he hadn't been home in so long there might already be one there and he wasn't any the wiser. On the rare times he'd called his mother, she never mentioned anything had changed. Buc-ee's would be a topic of conversation. Guilt slammed into him for the neglect he showed his family. Duncan Hayes was gone. As much as Tiernan didn't wish anyone harm, he couldn't muster a tear for his dear old grandfather, either.

The Cantor cabin was more like a lake house. It was an A-frame made from wood. There was a porch and a second-story balcony of almost equal size. The place was all windows and views.

"I thought you said this was a cabin in the woods," he said to Melody as he parked.

Her forehead creased as she shot him a look. "I haven't been here in so long. It seems smaller to me now."

"I get that you didn't want to use this place given its purchase history," he said, but he'd also picked up on something else in her tone when she mentioned it before.

"There's more to it," she said. "How about I tell you later?"

"We don't even have to talk about it if the subject makes you uncomfortable," he said. There was no need unless she felt like telling him what the tone in her voice was about. He'd picked up on the subtle sadness.

"I want to talk," she quickly countered. "Not with everyone. But I don't mind telling you. I actually haven't told anyone so much about my family and our relationship in such a long time." She paused for a second. Long enough to bite down on her bottom lip—lips that were in the shape of Cupid's bow and darn kissable. "Actually, I never discuss my family with anyone else. You're the first person to hear my side of the story."

He smiled at her before heading out of the truck. The fact she wanted to share her secrets with him caused more of that stirring in his chest that he'd been trying and succeeding in avoiding for many years up until now. He was clearly failing when it came to Melody. She was a rogue storm that blew into his life unexpectedly and without all the damage left behind. She was the good kind with lightning that cut across a velvet sky and thunder that caused the walls to rattle.

Then again, they would have to part ways at some point. The thought darn near gutted him. But what did he plan to do about it? Right now? Nothing.

Tiernan opened her door and then refocused on the cabin. The place was nice. There was a tire swing hanging from a large oak tree. He suspected there was a lake or some kind of water source nearby. He'd better keep an eye on Loki since he loved gunning straight for just such places, coming back drenched, muddy and happy as a lark. Or sprayed by a skunk. Tiernan never knew what he was going to get with his oversize pup but he could bank on trouble following.

"Watch out for tracks leading up to the house," he said to Melody. At this point it was later in the afternoon. The sun was out today, warming his skin. There was a chill in the air like nobody's business. His thoughts wandered to his own family and how they were doing. Seeing what Melody was going through with her family reminded him to be a better son. Other than Duncan, his family was loving. They were good people who cared about one another. Why was it so much easier to hate a jerk than to focus on the good people in his life?

"Okay," Melody said, checking the ground as she walked toward the A-frame. She spun around. "Do you think we should hide the fact we're here?"

"What did you have in mind?" he asked.

"Parking a little bit away from the house," she clarified. "I mean, I doubt my brother would show up here but he might send someone. My mother could show up at some point. I don't come here any longer and haven't for years so I have no idea what anyone's habits are."

"Good idea," Tiernan said. "Can you keep Loki with you?"

Loki had other ideas. He followed Tiernan back to the truck.

"Never mind," Tiernan said. "I'll take him with me instead." He paused at the door to his truck. "Do you want to come with us?"

"You'll only be a minute, right?" she asked.

"All I intend to do is park outside of view. Just up the lane a little bit," he said. "You should be fine until I get back."

"I grew up coming here," she said. "I still know this place like the back of my hand. Go on. I'm good here."

Tiernan climbed into the driver's seat after allowing Loki passage. The night at the vet's office did him good. The Lab had more energy than Tiernan had seen in a while, which was saying something.

There was a spot to pull off not too far from the A-frame that should keep the truck blocked from view. The good thing was that no one knew what Tiernan's truck looked like. Correction— Melody's brother would know if he'd been paying attention this morning. Coop had looked stressed out, so those details might have escaped him. The guy had been cagey, and Tiernan didn't pick up on one single warm vibe toward Melody. Would it be the same with his siblings when he visited home again? He couldn't imagine a world where the Hayes kids, grown as they might be, would turn against each other. Self-interest was the only vibe Tiernan had received from Coop. The guy could be a younger, more deviant version of Duncan, which probably didn't help much.

Tiernan was predisposed to not liking the guy

based on the association with his grandfather. Was it fair to put them both in the same bucket? Maybe not. Tiernan hadn't spent enough time around Coop to decide one hundred percent if his instincts about the guy were correct. But then, initial impressions were usually right.

Hiking back to the A-frame, Loki bolted. Not unusual for the pup, but the move was unsettling to Tiernan in this situation. His radar was already on high alert as it was. The last thing he needed was another reason to be stressed.

Rather than shout for his dog, he kept a low profile. If Loki took off too far, he would be bringing home ticks at the very least. The dog had a way of finding trouble, Tiernan was learning. So, he headed in the direction his dog had taken off to instead of the A-frame.

"Loki," he whispered.

When no dog came tearing through the woods, Tiernan whistled. Still nothing. He bit back a few curse words that would make Granny blush. Thinking about home earlier made him miss all the important people in his life. Or maybe it was the fact he seemed to be surrounded by death— death had a way of reminding people to live.

MELODY CHECKED THE ground for footprints leading up to the front door. This time of year, wind whipped the dirt around so she didn't expect to find any. Her assumption was correct. She wasn't sure exactly what to look for other than obvious signs, like a light being left on. Her brother hadn't washed a load of laundry in his life. There would most likely be dirty clothes in the master bathroom in a hamper. What else?

The front door was locked, which wasn't unusual. The planter still held the key. Sun reflected off the windows, making it impossible to see inside. Being back at this house after decades away, she had no idea what the place looked like any longer.

Walking inside was like stepping into a time capsule. Between the pair of long, white couches facing each other in the living room and the antler chandelier over a massive dining table next to the kitchen, not much had changed. The lamps even looked the same as she remembered. A white marble coffee table sat in the middle of the room. Two benches opposite each other along with the couches formed a loose box around the coffee table in the living room. The place was set up for entertaining. The dining table seated twelve. Happy memories from her childhood and teenage years came flooding back. Granted, they were pleasant because she had no idea what her family truly was at the time…a house of cards ready to be blown away by the first strong wind.

Brently's family had come here, too. This

room at sunset had housed their engagement party. Even then, during the height of her obliviousness to how bad her father truly was, there'd been a little voice in the back of her mind asking if Brently was *the one*. Was he comfort? Familiarity? The known?

Looking back, her heart never raced in the way it did when Tiernan was nearby. No one made her feel so out of control in a way that was exciting and comforting instead of scary. He'd been right by her side during this whole ordeal—an ordeal that needed to end with justice carried out.

Starting in the living room, there weren't any lights left on. The room was bright from the sun, so she methodically checked each bulb and light switch to be sure. Blankets had been tossed onto the sofas and not straightened, but that didn't exactly mean anything. There was a small, local cleaning service that used to come before and after family trips here. Did the pair of sisters still clean the house?

Moving into the dining room, nothing seemed out of place. There wasn't much inside this area except for a curio cabinet that housed dishes and a couple of decorative vases along with the large table and chairs. There were no signs of the room being disrupted in any way.

In the kitchen, there were no dishes in the

sink. She checked the dishwasher. None inside there, either. Of course, it stood to reason the cleaning ladies might have come and gone. Coop would never make the call himself, but Janice might. She'd probably stepped into the role of Melody's mother after the divorce. There was so much she didn't know about her own family now that she'd severed ties for the most part. It was an odd feeling. Mother, Coop, her sister-in-law, even her father were essentially strangers to her now.

The bathroom hamper was empty. Then, it dawned on her to check the fridge. The cleaners never threw out food if it hadn't expired. Melody made the trek back into the kitchen to check.

Halfway through the living room, a noise outside startled her.

"Tiernan?" she asked as she moved toward the sound. The front door was cracked open, and an uneasy feeling someone was watching her pricked the tiny hairs on the back of her neck.

Chapter Twenty-One

Tiernan trudged through the scrub toward the sound of Loki panting and twigs breaking. The dog was trouble times ten. It was a good thing Tiernan had an almost endless well of patience with animals. People, not so much. Except when it came to Melody. She was the exception to pretty much every rule he'd ever made and tried to enforce.

"Loki, come," Tiernan said with authority as Loki blew by.

The dog did an about-face and bolted back to Tiernan's side. He darn near fist-pumped the victory. Since he was turned around, he headed back toward where he believed the road to be, found it and then walked to the A-frame. By now Melody might have some sense of whether or not her brother had, in fact, visited like he'd said or if that was another in a growing list of deceptions.

The front door was cracked open, so he walked inside and glanced around.

"Melody," he called out.

There was no response. Tiernan's pulse jacked through the slanted roof. He probably should have brought his shotgun from home for protection but hadn't thought of it. Tiernan bit back a curse. Since he could see straight into the kitchen, he headed there for a weapon as Loki tore through the downstairs at almost full speed. All the rest he'd gotten at the vet's last night was causing him to bounce off the walls at this point. Tiernan wished he'd had time to throw the tennis ball to work off some of that puppy energy.

After locating a cleaver, Tiernan took the steps two at a time, doing his level best to be quiet. There was a small landing with several oversize beanbag chairs, and a pair of bedrooms with what looked like a Jack-and-Jill bathroom in between.

An animal-like grunt came from the room on the left. Tiernan bolted toward it with Loki jumping in front. Loki stopped. His ears came up, his hackles raised, and a low, throaty growl tore from his throat.

Tiernan moved to the side of the door frame before having a look inside. Melody sat on the bed. She had tape over her mouth, her hands and ankles were bound, and she was rope-tied to the bedpost. Every muscle in Tiernan's body corded. He had to suppress the instinct to run to her because whoever did this to her was nowhere in sight.

The second her eyes met his, she tried to warn him. She motioned toward the closet and then shook her head. Her wide fearful eyes were knife stabs. The coil in his chest tightened to the point of pain.

But it was the snick of a bullet being lodged in a chamber that came from behind him that demanded his immediate attention. He turned sideways so he could keep an eye on Melody.

"Hands up," came the sheriff's voice. Cleve Tanner stood on the landing.

Startled by the voice and the noise, Loki turned and barked. He didn't seem to know which way to fix his attention, committing to neither side.

Tanner had on jeans and a sweatshirt along with his boots. There wasn't a hint of law enforcement employment on anything he wore, which said a whole lot about his intentions.

Considering there was a gun pointed at him, Tiernan complied with the request. The second the sheriff saw the knife, he zeroed in on the center of Tiernan's chest with the barrel of his gun.

"Set the knife down on the carpet, along with

your cell phone," Tanner instructed. "Make a move that I don't like and all three of you are dead. Guess who'll go first?" He shifted the barrel to point at Loki.

Tiernan pulled on every ounce of self-discipline to refrain from charging at the sheriff to tackle him at the knees. Right now, Cleve Tanner had the upper hand. The lawman knew it, too. Once again, Tiernan complied, but he clamped his jaw so tightly that he feared his back teeth might crack. To hell with it.

He fished his cell from his pocket, and then slowly dropped down.

"Kick them toward me when you're done," the sheriff instructed.

"I don't know how you expect me to do that with a knife," Tiernan said, rolling his cell in the man's direction.

"Toss it," the sheriff said. "But if it hits me, your dog is the first to die."

Carefully, Tiernan chucked the knife. Fighting the urge to lunge at the sheriff, Tiernan slowly stood up.

"You're okay," he reassured Loki in as calm a tone as he could muster. A not-so-silent rage was boiling to the surface inside him. He was no match for a gun. This situation must have caught the sheriff off guard because there was no silencer. Tiernan put his hands in the air.

"What next, Sheriff? What do you plan to do? You couldn't kill us in my workshop."

"That wasn't me," the lawman said before seeming to catch himself.

Melody was going crazy in the next room, trying to communicate something. Loki's nerves were fried. The unpredictable pup was causing near cardiac arrest for Tiernan.

"Tie him up," the sheriff said as Loki looked on. His growl was enough to put fear in an MMA fighter. "And tell the woman to be still or I'll shoot you next."

Why the sheriff hadn't fired already dawned on Tiernan. An investigation could tie this place to the crime. There would be blood spatter everywhere. Too much to fully clean it all. The sheriff knew all the ins and outs. His DNA could be linked to the scene. It was amazing what forensics could do with a small hair sample in this day and age. Threats were one thing. Discharging the weapon was a different ballgame. So, Tiernan would have a little leeway.

The fire in the sheriff's eyes said he'd do it if that was the only way.

"I'm going to take a knee to calm my dog down," Tiernan said as he slowly lowered himself. This had the added benefit of making him a smaller target. Besides, if the sheriff shot at Loki, Tiernan had no qualms about taking the bullet instead. He held on to his dog by the collar. The move worked. Loki's tail was going a mile a minute but he stopped the rapid-fire barking.

"Shut her up now," the sheriff demanded.

"It's going to be okay, Melody," Tiernan reassured. He turned to her and winked to communicate he understood what she was trying to tell him. Someone else was there. The person hadn't made themselves known. Tiernan couldn't figure out the sheriff's involvement. What did he have to gain by implicating Melody? Why wasn't he investigating Coop?

"What's the endgame here, Sheriff?" Tiernan asked. By his count, the sheriff was outnumbered. Then again, Melody had indicated someone else was around. Was the person in the closet the mastermind behind this all? To what end? What was there to gain?

Tiernan's cell buzzed. The sheriff's muscles tensed. The screen was visible. John Prescott.

"You had to get other people involved," the sheriff said. "You couldn't leave well enough alone."

"He's on to you," Tiernan hedged. "And he's heading this way." The little white lie might force the sheriff's hand. "If I don't pick up, he'll be suspicious."

"How stupid do you think I am?" the sheriff

asked, shaking his head. "You answer and you'll give him some type of signal behind my back. I'm not stupid, Hayes."

"Speaking of last names," Tiernan continued. He saw how rattled the sheriff had become and how much he was trying to cover. It was the little things giving him away now. The twitch just below his left eye. The way his chest moved up and down a little faster because his breathing was shallow. A shot of adrenaline would do that to a person. "Mine is well known in this state. Do you think my family will accept my disappearance? My murder? Because I know they would move heaven and earth to find the person responsible for my death."

The sheriff needed to know the field he was playing in.

"Aren't you an elected official?" Tiernan asked. "You can kiss that job goodbye. But then, you'll be living in a cell anyway. Do you know what inmates do to former law enforcement officers?"

He still couldn't piece together why the sheriff would be involved in any of this. Cleve Tanner didn't strike Tiernan as being exceptionally bright.

"You'd better get out here, Mr. Cantor," the sheriff finally called out after a long pause. "This one is causing trouble, and you have to make a call as to what to do next. This is more than I'm getting paid for." The secret was out now. The sheriff was being bought off to set Melody up for murder. Getting rid of Melody would have made it impossible for her to defend herself in court. Murders that Coop Cantor had committed with a possible assist from a lawman.

Coop Cantor came flying out of the closet. "What the hell?"

Loki went crazy, lunging toward him. Coop backed up a couple of steps until his back was against the window.

"Call the dog off," Coop demanded. Sweat dripped from his forehead. His armpits were stained.

"Are you seriously planning to kill your own sister?" Tiernan asked as he stayed crouched low. "Because you'll never get away with it."

Coop shot a look that said he had the law on his side, and it was standing behind Tiernan with a gun aimed at his back.

"Have you ever killed someone?" Tiernan asked. "Because I have. It was an accident, but I still have nightmares. I still see Mary Jane's face when I close my eyes. Watch her drown all over again as I stood there frozen on the pool deck thinking that she was being silly and not taking her last breaths." The made-up story rolled off his tongue and seemed to be having the right effect. Coop shifted his weight as he white-knuckled the windowsill behind him.

"This situation is complicated," the sheriff said. "I didn't sign up for this. I did my part and you were supposed to handle the rest."

Tiernan wished he had his cell phone so he could record this conversation. It was too far away to reach. Any sudden movement would backfire. He had, however, managed to unclip Loki's collar. The studs on it could do serious damage wrapped around his fist as he delivered a punch. Get him close and he could take down the sheriff. Coop was strong and athletic. Not as fit as Tiernan, though.

The numbers were off. It was two against one since Melody was tied to the bed. One of them had a gun.

This tension in the room ratcheted up a few more notches with Loki going wild. Tiernan called his dog, noticing Loki had positioned himself in between Coop and Melody. Did the Lab mix have a protective instinct that Tiernan hadn't witnessed before?

"Shut the dog up," Coop demanded, his voice rising in panic. Panic wasn't a good thing except that it could serve as a distraction. The sheriff took a step closer to Tiernan. The man was almost near enough to spring toward and disarm.

Out of the corner of his eye, he saw that Melody had just freed her hands from the bedpost. Her movements were subtle and the chaos with Loki drew attention away from her.

In a flash, their gazes locked. Tiernan knew exactly what to do.

MELODY JUMPED UP, hopped a couple of steps, and threw herself at Coop. She'd worked her wrists free from the ties, ignoring the burn. A bullet split the air. There was no time to check for injuries or see if it hit a target. The window broke from the sheer force of his weight, and her brother fell backward with a shocked look on his face. He was half in, half out and trying to grab hold to keep from falling.

She might not know her family any longer but the same was true of them. They had no idea who she was or what she was capable of doing. She grabbed her brother by the legs. He tried to buck her off, but he nearly lost his grip and plunged to the ground. A fall like this one probably wouldn't kill him unless he landed wrong.

"What the hell, sis?" Coop asked. The last word came across like fingernails on a chalkboard after what he'd tried to do to her.

Since he was bigger, stronger and more athletic, she had to make a difficult decision. She picked up his legs and pushed as hard as she could.

"Are you trying to kill me?" Coop asked, surprise in his voice. And a little panic, too. One hand was gripping the frame while the other dangled outside.

With no time to waste, she leaned forward and bit his fingers. One last shove and her brother dropped like a hundred-and-eighty-five-pound bowling ball. Despite the bastard Coop had become, her heart hurt as she heard him scream out in pain at the landing. She risked a glance and saw that a bone had come through the leg of one of his trousers. He was alive, though.

Melody immediately turned in time to see Tiernan on top of the sheriff, squeezing him with his powerful thighs. The sound of a vehicle pulling onto the gravel drive twisted her stomach in a knot.

Chapter Twenty-Two

"We have company," Melody said while Tiernan squeezed his thighs harder as he pinned down the sheriff. Between Tiernan and Melody, they'd done well. They made a good team. One Tiernan wasn't quite ready to walk away from. They had company outside and he feared this fight was just beginning.

"Do you know how to shoot a gun?" he asked her. He could hold the sheriff if she could handle whatever walked up those stairs.

"No," she admitted. "I'm guessing it isn't that difficult."

"I can walk you through everything you need to know," he said, motioning toward where the Glock had flown after knocking it out of the sheriff's hand.

Loki bolted toward the open-concept stairwell. At least they would be able to see whoever walked through the door from this vantage point.

The dog might offer a distraction, a moment of hesitation that could give Melody a clear shot.

"Go over there," Tiernan said, motioning toward the opposite side of the landing. "Pop up, aim and shoot."

Melody nodded. Her hands trembled and there were red marks on her wrists. There were fifteen rounds in a Glock 19. One had been fired as Tiernan had wrestled for control of the weapon.

The sheriff tried to buck Tiernan off. He fired off a punch that sent blood shooting from the sheriff's nose. Sitting on top of a lawman while Melody had the guy's gun didn't look good. Of course, Tiernan wasn't expecting a deputy to walk through the door.

"Knock, knock." Prescott's voice was a welcomed relief coming from the front door.

"Don't shoot," Tiernan whispered.

Melody set the gun down and backed away from it. "We're in here and we're alive."

From their vantage point at the top of the stairs, they watched as the front door opened and the lawyer walked in.

"There's a mess up here," Tiernan immediately said.

"There's another one outside, too," Prescott said as Loki practically bowled him over.

"The sheriff is dirty," Tiernan explained as Melody kept far enough away to stay free of any wild arms or feet should any break loose. "And he's trying to knock the daylights out of me right now."

Prescott held up his cell phone. "Help is on the way. I already called for law enforcement and an ambulance."

"How did you know to come here?" Tiernan asked.

Prescott held up his cell phone. "Easy to track the sheriff's location with tech nowadays after attaching a small device onto his service vehicle. Couldn't figure out why on earth he would follow you guys here."

"Did he plant those notes, too?" she asked.

"My guess is they were going to tie back to you at some point, so, it's likely," Prescott confirmed.

Melody dropped to her knees and put her face in her hands. "It's over. It's really over."

All he wanted to do right now was haul her against his chest and be her comfort, claim those lips as his. Right now, she deserved answers.

The lawyer crested the top of the stairs with his cell phone in his hand. "I'm going to get a recording of this." He tapped the screen. "What you're seeing here is my client being victimized by law enforcement." He looked to Tiernan. "As a witness who had to subdue the sheriff, can you offer a statement as to what happened here?"

Tiernan gave a quick and dirty rundown of the events. Prescott asked Melody to do the same. She provided her side and her encounter with her brother. Prescott walked around the upstairs and the bedroom where the events took place.

"Sheriff, you're going away for a long time unless you start talking," Prescott said. "I can't guarantee that you won't anyway, but your co-operation will go a long way toward a more lenient sentence. Then again, you already know how this works, don't you?"

"I didn't kill anyone," the sheriff conceded. "I got paid to make sure the evidence led back to Melody Cantor."

"Why?" Prescott asked as Melody excused herself, no doubt to check on her brother. "What did Coop have to gain? There wasn't any family money, was there?"

"All I know is that he needed to get rid of anyone who could come after the family money. There were trust funds set up and he would get all the money if his half-brother and sister were gone. He didn't want to kill Melody at first. If she was a felon he wouldn't have to. Her inheritance would fall to him," the sheriff explained. "Then, everything started getting complicated when Tiernan got involved. Coop said she was going to be an easy target because she had no one to turn to."

"To be clear, you were paid off to look the other way for two murders, two attempted murders, *and* you were supposed to make sure the evidence for Jason's murder led back to Melody Cantor," Prescott surmised.

"Yes, sir. That sounds right," the sheriff admitted. This piece of human garbage needed to be locked up for the rest of his life. "The fire in the workshop was me."

"Your boot prints would have already been all over the area," Prescott deduced.

The sheriff nodded.

"Thank you," Prescott said as the sounds of sirens filled the air. He excused himself to meet law enforcement so he could explain the situation.

It took every ounce of willpower inside Tiernan to refrain from hammering the sheriff for the life he'd tried to destroy, the life of the woman Tiernan had fallen for. Greed was a disease in some folks. The sheriff must have seen Melody as his ticket to pad his retirement illegally.

A deputy came up the stairs within minutes. He took over for Tiernan, zip-cuffing the sheriff as another deputy removed the weapons and placed them in evidence bags.

"Why my land?" Tiernan asked, referring to burying Jason's body.

"It was a mistake to get you involved," the

sheriff stated with remorse. Not for a life lost but most likely because he got caught. "It was remote, and I rarely saw anyone on the road behind your property."

The miscalculation was responsible for the sheriff's arrest.

Tiernan glanced up at the deputy, who nodded and then took over. The second Tiernan was freed of his duty to sit on the sheriff, he bolted downstairs. The scene in front of him as he stepped outside made him fall in love with Melody all the more. She sat on the edge of the porch, her arm around Loki, comforting him.

"Hey," Tiernan said, not wanting to startle her. "How do you feel about having company?" He could only imagine how awful it must be to learn her own flesh and blood had set her up for murder.

"Hey," she said back. She had a surprising amount of composure under the circumstances. "Sure, come on and sit down."

He joined them, sitting beside her.

"I don't have words to say how sorry I am your own brother was willing to hurt you in such a horrible way," he started, wishing he could take away her pain.

"Remember this morning when you realized my brother's truck hood was warm and he denied going anywhere?" she asked. He took note she didn't address his comment.

"I do," he said.

"He'd dropped my sister-in-law off at the airport along with their bags," she said, staring out onto the lawn as, one by one, the emergency vehicles pulled away. "I'm guessing the only reason we caught him at home was because he had to go into the office like everything was normal. Janice was never in Dubai. She was headed to Brazil. Coop was probably waiting for word of my arrest after stealing a bracelet my mother gave me when I turned eighteen and planting it."

"The bastard deserves the prison sentence he'll get for orchestrating this," Tiernan said. He would give an arm if it could take away a fraction of the sadness in her voice right now. This might not be the time to tell her how he felt about her. Not while she was still reeling from losing the last tether to her family. "I don't know who used the ticket for the Longhorn game, but it couldn't have been him."

"Or the sheriff just planned to cover that up, too," she said with disgust.

Prescott, who had been sitting in his vehicle and taking notes, exited and walked toward them. He held his cell out in front of him. "There's someone on the line who would like to speak to you."

Melody blinked a couple of times but didn't respond or reach for the phone.

"It's your father," Prescott said. "Maybe hear him out."

Melody took in a deep breath before Tiernan looped his arm around her waist. She leaned into him, causing all kinds of fireworks to go off inside his chest.

"DAD," MELODY SAID after taking the offering.

"I'm sorry, Mellie," her dad said, reminding her of the nickname he'd called her most of her life before she walked away from the family.

"It was Coop," she clarified.

"I'm not talking about the ordeal you've just been through," he said. "I'm sorry for that, too. I owe you an apology for so much."

"Water under the bridge now," she said, not sure where this was going. "We don't have to rehash the past."

"I let you down and swore I would never do it again," he continued, unfazed. There was a kindness to his tone that she didn't recall ever being there. "I've had a lot of time to think recently, and all I can say is that I should have been the father you deserved. I wanted to be the person you looked up to when you were a little girl, Mellie."

Tears pricked the backs of her eyes at the admission.

"You stopped talking to us, to me, and I thought giving you space was for the best," he said. "But that wasn't fair to you, either. What I'm trying to say is that I'd like to become the person I saw in your eight-year-old eyes, and I'm just hoping I'm not too late."

A few rogue tears fell. She tucked her chin to her chest to hide the emotions spilling out of her eyes.

"It's hard, Dad," she said. "I want to believe you're different but I can tell you that I can't go back. You'd have to be honest with your dealings with me and everyone else before I could even consider it."

"I'll make the commitment right now if you'll promise to let me make this up to you," her father said.

She'd wanted to hear those words for so long. Could she trust him?

Tiernan's words came back to her. Without trust, she could never let anyone in, which sounded lonely. It was. It had been. And it was time for second chances.

"Okay," she said. "I'll try if you will."

"You've made me a happy father, Mellie," he said. She could hear the emotion welling up in his throat. "I have to go now. We'll talk soon."

"Sounds good, Dad," she said, betting there were hundreds if not thousands of grown women out there wishing they could have one more conversation with their father. Melody wouldn't waste this chance to let him make things right between them.

She ended the call and handed the cell phone back to Prescott.

"Your father asked me not to tell you this, but I refused because there's something you should know," Prescott said.

Melody cocked an eyebrow. "That is?"

"He's covering for your brother's actions. Coop was the one taking the money. Your father blindly signed off on the paperwork making him liable, and he refused to give his son up to the law. Said Coop was young and didn't belong behind bars for the rest of his life," Prescott said.

"Wait. What?" Melody couldn't hide her shock.

"I'm in the process of talking him into changing his plea. Now that he knows what Coop was doing with his freedom, your father is more inclined to come clean," Prescott informed. "Anyway, just thought you should know." He excused himself and disappeared first into his vehicle and then down the road.

Most people lived in a place somewhere between right and wrong. The gray area. Her father wasn't faithful in his marriage and that made the business dealings that much easier to believe.

She figured Coop was responsible for Jason's murder, too. Had he even made a visit to their father? Or had Coop interceded?

There had to be some good in her brother, too. It was lost. Buried underneath layers of ice. But, someday, she hoped the casing would melt and he would find himself again. In the meantime, he was going to have a lot of time to think.

And then there was the man sitting beside her. She couldn't let another minute pass without speaking her mind.

She turned into him and got comfortable in the crook of his arm. She couldn't look into his eyes when she said the next words in case he didn't feel the same.

"Tiernan Hayes, I've never met anyone like you," she began. "I could live a whole lifetime and not meet another one like you." Suddenly, her mouth dried up. She pushed through the nerves and the awkwardness that came with not being able to say the words perfectly to express her feelings. "What I'm trying to tell you is that I've fallen in love with you, and it's okay if you don't feel the same way. I just thought you should know and..."

That was as far as she could go. It was like running out of gas, and she couldn't force another word out of her mouth.

Tiernan brought his hand around to her chin. He lifted her face so that she was looking directly into his eyes. "I've met a lot of folks in my life, but it wouldn't matter if I hadn't. There was something in my heart that recognized you almost from the minute I first met you. Like lightning striking. It's taken a minute to seed because I kept trying to convince myself that I didn't know you. But somewhere deep down, my soul recognized yours. I'm in love with you, Melody. I don't want this to end. Ever. Does that scare you?"

"Those six words are music to my soul," she said. "Because I can't imagine being with anyone but you."

"I'd like to take you to meet my family," he said. "It's time for me to go home and make things right. Will you go with me? Stay with me? Be with me?"

"Forever," was all she said, all she had to say for him to lean in and kiss her so tenderly it robbed her of breath. He pulled back just enough, his lips still gently pressed to hers.

"That's a good place to start," he said, his mouth moving against hers.

For the first time in Melody's life she was right where she belonged, with Loki and Tiernan. She'd found her man, her dog and her home. And there was no other place she wanted to be than right here in Tiernan's arms.

* * * * *

USA TODAY *bestselling author Barb Han's*
The Cowboys of Cider Creek miniseries
continues next month!

And if you missed the previous titles
in the series, look for:

Rescued by the Rancher
Riding Shotgun
Trapped in Texas
Texas Scandal

You'll find them wherever Harlequin Intrigue
books are sold!